To Nick O'Nama
with best wishes

TIEGN
AND THE LIVING STONES

———•◆•———

JOHN MARGERYSON LORD

Order this book online at www.trafford.com
or email orders@trafford.com

Most Trafford titles are also available at major online book retailers.

© Copyright 2013 John Margeryson Lord.
All rights reserved. No part of this publication may be reproduced, stored in a
retrieval system, or transmitted, in any form or by any means, electronic, mechanical,
photocopying, recording, or otherwise, without the written prior permission of the author.

Printed in the United States of America.

ISBN: 978-1-4669-8226-0 (sc)
ISBN: 978-1-4669-8224-6 (e)

Library of Congress Control Number: 2013903648

Trafford rev. 03/28/2013

 www.trafford.com

North America & international
toll-free: 1 888 232 4444 (USA & Canada)
phone: 250 383 6864 ♦ fax: 812 355 4082

About this book

This story is pure fiction, and is one of three books about Stonehenge. The start of the construction of the monument we know today as Stonehenge is described in "BORK—And The Stones of Power", and the second book "PFINGER And The End of Power" illustrates its final abandonment. This small volume is about life around the period in between these two phases when Stonehenge was in mid construction.

Dedication

This book is dedicated to the very recent archaeologists who have conducted a new dig in and around the monument known as Stonehenge and whose findings completely support the use and purpose of the great stone circle as described in these stories.

The Characters

All the characters in this book are purely derived from my imagination and bear no relationship to any real person past or present. Any such likeness is purely coincidental.

The Sword Of Authority

Strictly speaking Stonehenge belongs to the Stone Age, but the building of it overlaps with the Bronze Age. The sword was unique and came from Central Europe where the skills of the worker in metal were just being developed. It was made especially for a very wealthy knight who brought it to Britain. The story of how the sword ended up in Tiegn's Clan is told in the companion book namely 'PFINGER—And The End Of Power'

CONTENTS

1. AN ENDING AND A BEGINNING..............1
2. THE BITTER TASTE OF SUCCESS 12
3. A SMOOTHLY RUNNING MACHINE........17
4. OPPOSITION..37
   4.1 The Dire Shape of An Aggressive Intent..40
5. ROONDOT — A LOOSE SWORD 55
   5.1 Power Mis-used..59
6. AN INTERLUDE..65
   6.1 A Growing Up...68
   6.2 Some Rivers Run Deep..............................74
   6.3 Reaction..79
   6.4 Loyalty Betrayed 81
7. WAR 83
8. AN AMUSING INTERLUDE 94
9. THE STRUGGLE GOES ON............................97
10. TIEGN TAKEN PRISONER..........................104
11. QUESTIONS AND A SEARCH....................108

12. A SECRET FORCE 113

13. AN ACCOUNTING 119

14. LIST OF CHARACTERS 125

15. ABOUT STONEHENGE 127

AN ENDING AND A BEGINNING

Tiegn gazed down at her father's crumpled features as he struggled for breath, her heart was wrenched in her breast. She loved him desperately, and not just because she needed him for his strength and his wisdom, but for his all embracing kindness. He was dying. He strained hard to speak and as he did so the small group standing beside the cot fell silent, for this was the moment they hoped that Pandil the dying man as the Chief of the Clan would name his successor. This was a long standing tradition. His son, Vandil, moved closer to the cot fully expecting that this heavy responsibility would fall to him. And so did most of Clan—All those present were about to be astounded by the old man as he struggled to speak.

His words when they came were clear enough.

'Vandil, son of my loins,' He managed between laboured breaths, 'One day you will be Chief. But your time is not now. You must be patient.' His fists clenched with the effort.

If that staggered the assembled group his next pronouncement stunned each and every-one of those present who heard it. There was no doubt as to his meaning.

And this is what, with increasing difficulty, he said—'I herby declare that my daughter

Tiegn shall be given the Sword of Authority and therefore from this very moment onwards she is our Clan Chief.' Here he stopped to gather strength. Then came his last speech on this earth. 'And may the ancestors guide her. I have decided on this choice and my decision is final. I know that you will give her the support she will need.'

During the shocked silence which followed this pronouncement the old one's laboured breathing gently ceased, and the Clan had a new Chief. And it was official.

History had been made.

The late Chief's now silent body was ignored as the group turned to Vandil and shook his hand with sympathy as if to say—'Never mind, we believe that he meant it to be you all the time. The Clan has never had a woman for Chief—it cannot be right.' But if that was what they thought they kept it to themselves.

Tiegn was equally stunned, but as she watched the group rally round her step brother, she knew just what their father had meant and it came upon her that it was now or never. She would be Chief. Her father had appointed her in true Clan tradition and she found in herself the determination to follow her father's sound government.

She faced the gathering and raised her hand for silence—and go it.

It was clear that they all expected her to announce her resignation—But they got another shock.

Tiegn and the Living Stones

The memory of this moment would haunt them for the rest of their lives. They turned to face Tiegn hardly daring to breath.

Gathering all her strength, and in the knowledge that what she did next would define her future, Tiegn drew herself up to her full height and said very quietly but with all the force she could muster —

'Now — here at my father's death, and you all clearly heard him, I have been declared Chief of the Clan, in line with the Clan's true traditions I therefore see that we all have no choice other than to accept his pronouncement. So here then as Chief are my first requests.'

She paused briefly to let this be understood. Then —

'Firstly . . . . , my father's body is to be prepared for burial at the place he chose when alive, and I ask my brother here to see that this is done. Tomorrow, when the sun is at its height my dear father will be laid to rest according to our traditions, and the entire Clan will be invited to attend. Following this, and at a suitable time, and with the appropriate ceremony the Sword of Authority will be handed to me by my nominated Deputy — Lakiln. This will be my formal acceptance of the Chieftainship of this Clan.'

She watched to see their reaction and was gratified to note that most looked relieved. This was what they were used to — a Clan Chief taking control and giving instructions. Things might not be so bad after all.

'In the meantime anyone who feels that this is not right and that my father did not know what he was doing can see me for a discussion, but I will not give up this responsibility.' She added.

Then in a less authoritative tone—'Now if you will be good enough to leave us I would like to have some time alone with my father.

'And as he would have wished it, we both thank each one of you for being here, at my father's end.'

They left slowly muttering between themselves. All, that is, except her brother. When there was only the two of them she faced a very angry Vandil—'You will never get away with this.' He hissed. 'I will fight you all the way. We both know that the job should have been mine.' And with that he turned away and strode out of the hut.

And the very first woman Clan Chief was totally alone.

Very alone.

Then when the others had left her to mourn her father Tiegn began to reflect on the legacy which she had so recently inherited from the dead man.

Her father Pandil had taken over as Clan Chief nominated by his father at his death and he similarly was young—barely a man. It was as the Clan tradition. Fortunately for Pandil the Clan was in the middle of a peaceful time.

Tiegn and the Living Stones

There had been a lengthy period of several cycles of good weather, and there was no shortage of food, and conflicts had been few and far between.

The work on the stones however did come to a halt during Pandil's period of office, causing him to have some difficult decisions to cope with, and he only just managed to survive.

It started off as a thin cloud on the horizon with nothing to indicate that it would gather into a vast stormy cloud, which filled the sky.

Surprisingly they had little or no problems with the setting up of the double ring of giant stones and their lintels, although there were still a number of these still being shaped before being lifted into their designated positions.

However, there were a number of smaller stones lying in a partial circle. These had been lying around unplaced for a considerable time. Several previous Chiefs had failed to decide what to do with these 'foreign' elements. The main rings of stones had reached the stage when these smaller stones had to be moved in order that none of the big stones would need to be moved again when setting the small ones in position.

One of the three men appointed by Pandil's predecessor to oversee the layout of the circles claimed to have contacted the ancestors and insisted that they had advised him that these small stones should play no part in the layout and they should be moved and taken away.

However the second man of the three said that the ancestors had told him that they were

Tiegn and the Living Stones

just as important as the big ones and should form a smaller circle inside the big stones.

When the third man was asked he claimed that the ancestors would not say where the stones should go but if we got it wrong there would be bad weather for a very long time. They could not afford to delay a decision.

To help picture the problem a layer of sand had been placed on the floor of Pandil's hut and stones were set in the appropriate places to represent the real ones. Other smaller stones lay in an untidy heap nearby waiting for a decision as to where they should be placed.

It was built into the rules of the Clan that Pandil could simply decide. But would he be right? And what would result from getting it wrong?

It was a previous Chief that had moved some of the stones into the great circles where they now lay. But he stopped with the work incomplete as misfortune in the shape of illness caused him to think again and leave well alone. Rumours were circulating as to the lack of benefit to be derived from these smaller stones.

So Pandil took up the challenge, and called the three advocates to account.

First was old Spell—He claimed prior knowledge of the original intentions and he was convinced that the earlier incomplete circle should be finished by using the remainder of these stones.

This, he argued, was obviously the intention and the work should be finished.

Wellan—a younger and more worldly-wise man claimed that these stones were no longer vital to the purpose of the structure. They had clearly had no effect on the outcome of the deliberations with the ancestors in the recent past, and therefore they should be removed completely before they were hemmed in by the completed ring of big stones.

Salleten—the youngest and more reactionary of the three, voiced an opinion that they should simply be left alone for some later chief to assume responsibility for the layout, thus completely avoiding the need for a decision. Should they get in the way of the big stones the awkward ones could easily be moved and later replaced.

Most of the ordinary Clan's folk did not have a view as to the eventual outcome, but since the decision did involve work and thus manpower they did require a clear mandate. Pandil was tempted to leave the problem until there was a pressing need for a decision, but his sense of his responsibility would not let him have it on his conscience for the rest of his life. He tried consulting with the ancestors—the result was a deep silence. He felt that they really didn't care.

So—After much thought he decided that the final decision should be the responsibility of the whole tribe. Thus he invented a procedure which had never been previously attempted and he was unsure as to the Clan's reaction. The plan was laid before his deputy but the man fought shy of voicing an opinion.

Tiegn and the Living Stones

In the end Pandil felt sure that it was the right thing to do.

He took his proposition to the ancestors and after a long and tiring session he concluded that they were broadly in favour of his plan.

Pandil called a Clan meeting, the first of his chieftainship.

There was a clear blue sky, and a yellow sun warmed the stones. The heat at mid-day was ameliorated by a light breeze gently stirring the leaves. It was ideal weather for such an important gathering. It was also a slack time in the fields and people had a little free time.

It took some little while for all to arrive at the stones, Pandil had insisted that the meeting was of prime importance so he waited until the last of the late comers had arrived. Only the sick and the very old and the very young were exempt.

As they arrived at the great stone circle Pandil was surprised and gratified that there was such a good turn-out. As the last arrived he addressed the gathering.

'Friends,' he began. 'I have called you all here to join with me in concluding a major decision about these stones.'

He waved a hand around behind him indicating the partial ring of smaller stones.

'We need to decide what to do with them.'

'In previous discussions I have been advised of three choices.'

'Each suggestion has its advocate, and so I will ask each of these three men to present their case for your consideration. When you have heard all three proposals I will take each of you in turn and ask you to go and stand with the man who presented the solution you favour. You are not obliged to choose but we do need to have a conclusion to which most of us agree. The proposal with the most people will be adopted.'

'In the case of an equal number I will add my own choice to one of them.'

Pandil paused to let the resulting swell of discussion die down, and was gratified that no one left the gathering. The general feeling was one of mild approval. Pandil felt that they were sufficiently intrigued to stay and join in the fun.

He then turned to old Spell and asked him to state his case.

A few in the crowd were enjoying themselves. Spell was encouraged—

'Tell us a good story old man.'

'Go on make us laugh, we need a good laugh.'

Nervously at first and then with growing confidence as the crowd listened politely to what he had to say, Spell put his case.

And it was the same with Wellen and Salleten who each gave their view.

Then Pandil called for quiet and asked for the people to choose who to stand with.

There followed a general mele as the Clan's folk wandered about to stand with the right choice. It was immediately clear to all that the biggest crowd stood with young Salleten, who looked quite pleased with himself. A short discussion between Pandil and his deputy followed. Then turning to the crowd Pandil announced that there was a big majority for Salleten's case to leave the stones alone—and this plan would be adopted.

To show their feelings at being involved in a major decision the gathering clapped, and voiced their approval.

A happy Clan gradually drifted off talking, even arguing amongst themselves.

Several people slapped a mighty pleased Salleten on his back.

Tiegn remembered all this and the pleasure that it gave Pandil to have succeeded.

'I too will leave those stones where they lie,' she said to herself.

Yes, on the whole Pandil's Chieftainship had been a success.

It was as she was considering these past actions that Tiegn began to realise that her father's decision to make her Clan Chief was no sudden spur of the moment thing forced upon him by his approaching death. He had in many different ways done his best to prepare her for this responsible office. He invariably involved her in any dispute and would even ask her just what action she would recommend. Should her expressed view differ from his Pandil would take the trouble to explain his own conclusion, which sometimes led to a lengthy debate. Tiegn began to learn the rules of fairness and to put her own sentiments to one side if doing so led to the right outcome.

He had insisted that, even when she was engrossed in some other activity, she joined him in private visits to the stones where he schooled her in the formalities and procedures involved in the complex business of communicating with their ancestors. In this way she got to know who they were talking to and what weight to place on very different subjects. One day it might be asking for help with a sickly child. Another day it might be an appeal for better weather. In this way she got to know and to respect them.

There was not an official action or ceremony in which he had not involved her. He did all this in such a normal manner that it was not obvious. Even her step-brother Vandil accepted their father's close relationship with Tiegn as being natural.

Her father had, she now realised, right from the first moment of her birth schooled he for the job of Clan Chief.

And with this realisation came a deep concern that she must not let her father down. Put simply—she must do the job and do it well. He was now with the ancestors and would be watching her.

THE BITTER TASTE OF SUCCESS

It should not be like this. The thought was torn from her mind by the searing crash of thunder as it echoed around the great stones, There was no pause as thin loose strands of lightening flickered around the place turning dark night into a terrible scene of shuddering shadows. The mind numbing noise was almost continuous preventing as it did any attempt at clear thinking and destroying any idea she had of sleep.

She went over her problem for the hundredth time. It seemed to be simple enough, her father had taken his last breath a number of days ago, and as he lay waiting patiently for the end he had named his eldest child, that is herself to be the next Clan Chief. It was of course the usual procedure and it had worked well for many generations. However, this time it was different—they had never before had a woman nominated as Clan Chief. It had simply never occurred. It was not that it was against any rule—there were none—it had simply never been done. It had never even been considered. Her father's command had come as a wholly unwelcome surprise and had already begun to show signs of splitting the clan. There were those who were declaring that they were solidly against having a woman as Chief, and there were those who considered that if the previous Chief had nominated someone then that someone, be they male or female, should be Chief, and the wishes of the outgoing Chief aught to be carried out without question. But significantly it appeared that the main body of the clan were undeclared. They required time to decide. Time in which they would be able to asses Tiegn's ability to hold down the Chieftainship.

Matters were due to reach crisis point on this coming day. As the sun reached its zenith the new Clan Chief would be presented to the clan and declared to be its Chief in a short ceremony before the stones and the Clan's ancestors when she would be presented with the Sword of Authority. Thus Tiegn as a female Clan Chief would be making Clan history. This ceremony had been arranged in spite of those whose voices had been raised in loud and bitter opposition.

Anxiety and the crash of the storm robbed her of sleep. She was unafraid for herself but deeply troubled as to the effect it would have on the cohesion of the Clan, which her father had maintained so successfully during his long tenure.

These dismal thoughts were frequently shattered by a storm that continued to rent the air unabated, and seemed at times to move the very earth. She knew that it would be taken by some as an omen that things should have been

Tiegn and the Living Stones

different and that it boded ill for her future Chieftainship.

It caused her great pain to find that her brother Vandil, just two seasons younger than herself, felt strongly that it should have been him as the male heir, to have been their father's choice. All his short life he had taken strength from the assumption that this would be his inheritance.

He had thought that it could not possibly have been otherwise. He could not have believed that such a dreadful thing could happen. But he, and the others present had heard it clearly and directly from their father's dying lips. All this was denying her the blessing of sleep to Tiegn as the troubled dawn approached.

Her overriding thought however was that if it had been her father's wish that she should serve the clan as its Chief—then her first duty was that she should obey him in his death as she had obeyed him in life.

The storm quietened as the feeble sun broke the horizon to revealed the ring of massive erect stones as they stood dripping under a watery grey sky. Sounds of the Clan emerging from the night reached Tiegn as she prepared to face her ordeal. She mentally thanked the ancestors for the day and asked for their help. It was as her father had schooled her.

A familiar voice outside her hut asked to enter, and the man who was to be her deputy greeted her with a grin. His cheery smile was a welcome contrast to her night's disturbing thoughts. She knew that she could not have wished for a better choice, Lakiln's unwavering support had been a mainstay of her father's reign, and this was now promised to her. With him she felt that she was not totally alone.

Lakiln immediately set to and organised the helping women to dress her and bring food and a hot drink to sustain her during this — the ceremony which would confirm her authority before the whole Clan.

But before the ceremony began she would try one more time to make peace with Vandil. It had been her idea to appoint him Lakiln's right hand man and to declare him as 'Clan Chief In Waiting' to become Chief automatically should anything happen to prevent her carrying out her duties. A churlish Vandil had accepted the job with very bad grace. His motives for doing so were not wholly loyal. It was in this turgid atmosphere that Tiegn was to assume her responsibilities.

In the event it proved to be far from easy. It brought the Clan to the very edge of extinction with revenge, traitors and even murder.

However, progress on erecting the stones had been excellent during her father's rule and there remained only four of the great upright stones and their associated lintels to be erected to complete the main ring.

After this, only the problem of re-sighting of the circle of smaller stones was required to finish what their ancestors had envisaged and had begun all those many generations ago. And this would now be left to a future Chief.

A SMOOTHLY RUNNING MACHINE

It had been a long and hard struggle to arrive at this point. In the beginning survival had been everything. Bork and his army from the north had attempted to stop them and to return to the old ways of following the herds and surviving by hunting and collecting fruit and vegetables when available, but he had been defeated.

Now, after so very many seasons since they began the massive construction, no-one in the clan could recall just why this place had been chosen for this new experiment in living, except that the ground seemed to have the right attributes in which to grow food-stuffs from seed for the first time. And to farm crops which could be relied on each year to support a growing population of workers and helpers whose dedicated efforts shaped and raised these stones which now overshadowed everything.

However, still in living memory was one who had been a babe when the founders of the Great Circle were alive. Sonlith, whose faith in the power of the stones had always governed the principles of his life. The ancestors whose lives were embodied in the stones were his guide—and his life and beliefs were taken by the Clan as a model on with which to base their own code of ethics. Without his dedication and strength when under formidable pressure, the group of huts which was the largest collection of permanent living quarters in either the Northern or the Southern Realm of Kingdoms would not exist and the members of the Clan would still be wandering loosely over the countryside.

There had been many hurdles to overcome.

Firstly and most importantly there were the stones. They were discovered lying scattered over a wide area, and were not of an appropriate shape to perform the function planned for them. It took a score of men with imagination and foresight to mark on the ground the position that each stone was to occupy. These huge chunks of virgin rock were then shaped and stood on end to form a double circle, the inner ones of which would be linked by massive horizontal lintels. It was intended to be the biggest and the most impressive of the many circles that had began to be built wherever people had decided to put down roots.

It would be the start of a new way of living.

Behind these stones was the belief that they held the spirits of their ancestors who would ensure the Clan's well being, and as such the stones represented a communication path to the passed ones. Their ancestors were honoured in loose ceremonies which took place at specific times which were closely related to the seasons.

Without this the group would certainly lack the cohesion it needed to survive as a Clan.

Tiegn and the Living Stones

Probably the most important and privileged members of the Clan were those men who carved, moved, and raised the stones to rest in their allotted positions. These men were revered and highly respected. Their work was hard and they were a very committed group. They generally began to learn their trade early in life, with sons following hard on the heals of their fathers.

Their toil did not allow time or energy for them to provide food for themselves or their families. So this had to be supplied by those who concentrated on the land and what it could produce. In this manner all the food available was gathered and then divided equitably amongst the entire Clan. Naturally in the course of events there were disputes, and these were brought to the Chief who heard each plea and ruled, his decision in these matters being respected and final.

Thus every able bodied person had a role to play in the survival of the Clan and in the construction of the great circle of stone which was their very foundation.

In the recent past and as Tiegn was yet to be born, and more than half complete, the circle had already become famous throughout the occupied lands. Its powerful message was being broadcast by the Story Singers. These individuals roamed the lands in small groups, as few as two and as many as four or five, picking up news and passing it on by means of songs. They would be welcomed housed, and fed by the Clan for their

Tiegn and the Living Stones

stay, and would move on after an evening of story telling, having picked up new information to be passed on.

The story now moves to the middle of Pandil's rule as Chief.

A visit from the Story Singers was a big occasion, And news of the possibility of such a treat had arrived. The Singers had heard of the work being undertaken to create an enormous ring of monumentally large stones, and were very keen to see the thing and Clan prepared to receive them.

It was the middle of the hot season of long days and the weather was settled and fine, perfect for the much anticipated visit.

The Singers were met by Clan Chief Pandil, and provided with food, whilst the Clan built and lit a bonfire in the centre of the living huts where the giant stones formed a stern background to the scene. They had carried the elderly and the unwell and placed them at the front—they were determined that none of the Clan should miss this rare party.

The Singers, a man and a woman, were finally seated by the fire. In contrast to the members of the Clan their skin was burnt almost black from travelling for many days exposed to all kinds of weather.

They were in fact a good deal younger than their appearance suggested, especially the woman.

But their general disposition was one of friendliness as they smilingly made a point of saying 'hallo' to the children who had been

Tiegn and the Living Stones

allowed to stay out on this very special occasion. As they took their place facing the Clan's folk the chatter gradually ceased and they were warmly introduced by the Chief, who took advantage of a period of relative quiet.

When this formality had been accomplished, the tallest of the man and wife team, in this case it was she, began . . . .

'Thank you for your welcome and the most enjoyable food. In return we will tell of some new things and some old ones.

She paused . . . .

'Firstly a very strange song about a very weird thing . . . .'

The pair then began to sing with an unusual and wavering melody — redolent with fear —

> 'On a cold and moonlit night,
> The whole Clan taken with a terrible fright.
> Out of nowhere appeared a tall and terrible shape.
>
> With blood dripping from its open jaw,
> A sight at which they could only gape,
> Unlike either man or beast was the thing they saw.'

At this she stopped. There was a stunned and total silence from the Clan.

Then, in a fearful tone—she sang—

> 'The thing took a branch from the fire,
> And plunged it into its heaving chest,
> It vanished in a shower of sparks
> It was a most unwelcome guest.'

A silence greeted this song's ending to be followed by an explosion of sound as the Clan reacted to the weird tale that had just been sung. They had no way of knowing whether it was true or not and were about equally divided on the matter. The singers gave nothing away, but began another song, this time striking a more cheery note. They took each verse in turn.

> Man: 'We have travelled far and wide,
> Visiting many in the countryside,
> Some of them are full of life,
> Others are having to deal with strife.'

> Woman: 'It seemed to us that the ones that were well,
> As far as that which we could tell,
> Had built their huts to last a storm,
> Neatly built and very warm.'

Tiegn and the Living Stones

> Man: 'The message here then is very plain,
> If its peace you wish to gain,
> Leave the stones that make your ring,
> Build good huts that is the thing.'

> The woman then suggested that they all join in with:—

> 'Leave the stones that make the ring,
> Build good huts that is the thing.'

This was generally appreciated by one and all and the chorus was re-sung several times. The singers then launched into some news gleaned from visits to several local sites. Most of the songs described incidents which were already known to the Clan but were much enjoyed when turned into song.

The fame of the ring of stones was being spread far and wide. The Singers told them that nowadays wherever they went people wanted to hear about this place and its giant and staggeringly impressive ring of stones. Above all they wanted to know if it conferred any obvious benefit to the Clan.

To this the singers replied by singing a song which they always did when being asked these questions.

Together, and in a sweet harmony—

> A visit to this place was always a joy,
> The air was clear and full of Peace,
> Every man, woman, girl and boy—
> Worked well and did not cease
> Until their allotted ask was done.
> And in this way each day was won.
>
> What made each person take their part,
> And give themselves to their tasks,
> Which they did with all good heart,
> There was no force that we could see,
> It seemed that they had their own reward
> From completing work however hard.

The message behind this song was not missed and they were rewarded by cheers. and applause. They then embarked on a song with a humourous theme.

> Living in a nearby place,
> Was a person in disgrace,
> Avoided whenever seen,
> He smelled because he wasn't clean.

Tiegn and the Living Stones

> Then one day in love he fell,
> But she pushed him down a nearby well,
> To make him fit to be seen,
> But out he came very green.
>
> The well you see,
> Just happened to be,
> A dumping place for all the lot,
> Of rubbish dumped down there and left to rot.
>
> The man was heard to give a curse,
> His smell you see was now much the.

This short piece had everyone laughing. The character in the song was well known, and they all knew that it was a true story.

The singers then sang some nursery songs which were much appreciated by the children who afterwards gradually drifted off to get a good night's rest.

It was now quite dark and the travellers wanted their own well earned sleep. Pandil thanked them which was the sign that things were finally at an end. An almost full moon lit the paths as the throng gradually dispersed and soon all that was left was the occasional crack from the dying embers of the fire. The great ring of stones cast their long shadows and were silent.

Tiegn and the Living Stones

The following day the singers requested to stay on to witness the planned activities, and in this they were welcomed by the Chief, with a warning not to get in the way.

Pandil then reviewed the work for the day, and on this occasion he felt a huge responsibility rested on his broad shoulders. It was to be a major event—they were about to raise and set into its final position one of the last of the big stones. It was the culmination of many, many days of hard toil, and if it all went well there would follow several days of thanks and celebrations. After this they would begin to prepare the next big stone, and do it all over again. But this did represent a significant moment in the building of the Stone Circle to which they were all committed. Above all—their ancestors would be honoured by the work.

The whole Clan was up and about as the sun broke the horizon and flooded the scene with brilliant light. The day was fine and stable as had been predicted by Salin, their reputed seer.

There was an air of excitement about as today had a great purpose. The story singers, having stayed on, found that they had to be careful not to get in the way as the serious work began.

When everyone had breakfasted the clan members not involved in the work, mainly the women and children began to form a loose circle of expectant watchers. They stood looking at an enormous rectangular stone which lay flat on its long side at the base of a man-made hill. This ramp terminated abruptly on the edge of a square pit which had been carefully dug precisely in line with those other stones which were already set in place, and in the shape of an arc of a great circle.

The stone lying on the ramp showed the clear marks where it had been worked on to give it the smooth shape it now owned. For many sun rises these hardy men working in all kinds of weather had dressed the great stone. Strong ropes and long wooden poles to be used as levers lay beside the thing. The gang leader shouted an order and two horses were led out and ropes fastened to a rope harness on each horse one on each side of the stone. Then when the whole Clan was assembled the leader took his position on a piece of raised ground where he would have clear view. At a sign from him men took hold of the ropes and the poles, dug their heels in and waited for the signal. When the leader was satisfied that all was ready he raised an arm which held a piece of white cloth. Paused for a moment and as he dropped his arm he yelled loudly—

'ALL TOGETHER—NOW—PULL.'

For a moment or two—nothing seemed to be happening as men and horses strained their utmost.

The leader yelled. 'PULL FOR THE SAKE OF THE ANCESTORS—NOW HEAVE.' Then quite suddenly the huge stone moved about a

Tiegn and the Living Stones

hand's width up the slope—its travel being made easier by the animal grease that covered the wooden rails on which it sat. This was greeted by a ragged cheer from the watchers. At this it stopped and a wooden stake was driven into the ground to prevent it returning down the slope.

The men relaxed, and rubbed their muscles, whilst the women moved amongst them with containers of water. It was clearly going to be thirsty work.

Thus, encouraged by the watchers, the leader signalled for the next pull, and the stone moved another hand's width. And so, with the crowd cheering every move, the stone crept gradually, hand's width by hand's width, up the slope.

The men and the horses were getting very tired and in spite of all the encouragement were clearly coming to the end of their strength, the last move had been but half of the earlier ones. The leader called a halt.

It was about mid-day and very warm. But they had not yet finished. Food and drink was brought and the team sat and ate where they had stood.

Now the stone was resting with nearly half its length overhanging the hole which was to be its home. Everyone realised that just a couple more good pulls and the thing would tilt and hopefully slide front end down into the hole, at which point it should rest in a nearly upright position leaning against the side of the hole. It then only remained for it to be hauled into an upright position.

Tiegn and the Living Stones

So, having satisfied hunger and thirst and now being rested, the gang took up their positions again and readied themselves for the final heave.

It took just two.

Then the huge stone seemed to move of its own accord and it very slowly stood up for the first time—and thankfully when it had stopped moving it was nearly upright.

A couple more heaves to ensure that the stone would not fall back, and the leader called a halt.

This was greeted by a great shout.

The leader bowed on behalf of the team and raised his hand and called for quiet—he now had to check that the huge stone was in the correct position and lined up with those already in place. It was a critical moment.

The means of ascertaining this was a special piece of rope with a set of knots along its length. Each knot represented a particular distance along the ground to be checked. The crowd and especially the team held their breath.

Suddenly the leader re-appeared from behind the stone. It was his moment.

He would be either feted or cursed.

He raised the white rag and shouted a single word.

—'CORRECT'

An enormous cheer filled the scene as the leader and his team danced and sang with relief.

There was still some hard work to do but another great stone had been set in its proper place to contribute its part to the giant ring which was slowly reaching completion. Another great step towards the final great circle had been taken.

That night was memorable for the celebrations. The story singers had created a song which made heroes of the leader and his team whilst making it clear that everyone in the clan had played their part in the achievement.

Clan Chief Pandil was cheered many times.

It had been a great day. A day to be remembered.

The splendid weather persisted through the next few days allowing work to continue both on the stones and on the crops. In addition a small group of five men checked their weapons and set off to find some game.

Back to where the newly erected stone was still leaning against the bank of soil a dozen or so strong individuals were busy tying ropes round the stone near its top. After a short break for some nourishment they collected as many men as they could find and be persuaded to help. At the stones they each took a rope and pulled it taught. Then at the shout of 'pull' they pulled. Very slowly the stone started to move, and quite suddenly was dead upright. One man then went round the stone with the knotted string to check that it had not moved out of position. Next he held a string on the loose end of which was fastened a small pebble. With the free end held against the great stone and the small one left to dangle, one could tell if the big one was upright or still leaning.

And after a short conference they declared it to be in the right place and perfectly upright.

This statement was greeted by a cheer from a fair crowd that had gathered to watch. And the Story Singers were there to witness this great success.

That night the Clan would celebrate this achievement and tomorrow there would be a ceremony of thanks. Then the team finished the job with the final task of packing in the loose earth around the base of the stone. They then retired to rejoin their families and friends, whilst the leader stayed by the newly placed stone and after placing his hand on it he spoke his own special thanks to the ancestors for the privalidge of a successful job.

His name was Keenly and it would be remembered.

Early the following day the Chief Pandil was out just before dawn. He strode slowly to the newly erected stone. He then placed certain objects on a nearby table sized block which had been moved into position, and began to murmur a private message of thanks. This would take some time during which most other Clan members and the Story Singers greeted the rising sun and made their way to the stones.

Eventually the Chief stopped and waited patiently until the normal chatter of greetings became silent. When all was quiet except for the loud piping of a solitary wren, the Chief proclaimed the newly laid stone to be part of the whole ring.

He then set fire to some piles of powder and a cloud of green and then red smoke rose into the still air.

'We thank our revered ancestors for their help and guidance during the preparation and raising of this latest addition to the ring. And we pledge to respect and cherish all that they stand for.

He raised his arms and conducted those present—

'We the members of this Clan thank our ancestors for their help, guidance, and support in all that we do.' The words rang out in the stillness of dawn.

And the ceremony was at an end.

Slowly the people dispersed to get on with their normal activities which had been so dramatically interrupted.

The Singers found their way to the Chief's hut and declared themselves duly impressed by all they had seen.

In response the chief advised them to stay and watch the stone masons at work preparing the next big stone, and after that, see what was being achieved in the grass lands to provide food to be shared by everyone in equal measure.

They thanked him and proceeded to find the path the Chief had indicated which led to where the next stone was being prepared.

———◆•◆•◆———

Tiegn and the Living Stones

The path took them through some tough woodlands until some considerable distance from the living areas they came upon a sizable clearing in the centre of which lay a stone much the same size as the others already in place in the ring.

Round it stood five or six strong looking individuals using a variety of tools to chip small fragments off the big stone. The ground around was covered with these chippings. I did not take them long to appreciate the skill and dedication of these men set to do this work day following day. The men did not pause but merely nodded to the Singers to acknowledge their presence.

Impressed the Singers returned to the Clan's gathering of huts.

On their way the Singers met the chief, and told him of their admiration of these dedicated men, And that they were about to compose a song in their honour which they would present that night.

As darkness crept over the scene, the bonfire was re-lit and the clan slowly gathered as before. The singers arrived just as the sun was sinking out of view.

The Chief called for quiet, and got it. He then waved to the Singers to start.

The male singer first waved his hand and in a serious voice full of emotion began.

Tiegn and the Living Stones

'We both wish to offer our very heartfelt thanks for the wonderful hospitality you have all shown us. We will tell it wherever we go.

Then in harmony they sang —

> 'We have travelled far and wide,
>   through woods and, over hills.
> And in all that we have seen of
>   people with many skills,
> Were nothing as compared with
>   those we saw today,
> These men who all day long
>   chipped the unwanted stone
>   away.
> Such men have to be extremely
>   tough,
> To do a job that is so rough,
> We can but admire and honour
>   them'
> We will but cherish and honour
>   them.

The Clan picked up these last two lines and sang them back loudly to the Singers who grinned and clapped in appreciation.

> 'We can but admire and honour
>   them,
> We will but cherish and honour
>   them.'

Tiegn and the Living Stones

At this the singers made it clear that this was the end of their offering and thanked everyone present for listening.

The following day the singers, who had discussed the matter between themselves asked the chief how the stone masons got fed as they had no time to provide for themselves.

The chief explained that all food was shared.

'Are there no arguments?' The woman asked.

The Chief's reply was to invite them to an argument that had just been raised, and which had to be sorted out.

So they strode over to the chief's hut in which two women stood as the Chief entered.

There were five others present two men and three women.

Pandil then explained that these were witnesses there to see that any ruling was fair to both complainants.

The Singers were welcomed and were asked to be seated near the back.

The Chief then nodded to one of the women to begin. She was the one raising the problem.

'Chief,' she began, 'This woman (she said her name) will not give up any of the twelve eggs that her hens have laid, hens which I (she gave her name) have fed from my own stock of corn.'

'Is this so?' Asked Pandil.

Tiegn and the Living Stones

'Yes it is — these eggs are not for eating they hold chicks to replace those hens I lost in that small fire we had. And I need them.'

The Chief then in whispers consulted one of the observers.

Turning to the owner of the hens, he said —

We remember that fire and we noted at the time that it was caused by your small son playing about with a burning stick. Is that not so?'

'Yes sir.' Was the reluctant reply.

The Chief consulted the observer again.

'Right! Since the fire was your responsibility you should give up the eggs, but we appreciate that you need to keep enough hens to continue with. Therefore you will select four of the best eggs which have been fertilised to provide you with four hens which will eventually give you more hens. The rest you will hand over for distribution. Further if any those you have given up produce chicks, those chicks will be yours also.'

'That is it, you may go.' He added.

At this both women expressed themselves to be satisfied with the ruling.

The story singers were duly impressed and said so.

Later as they finally left the Clan, the Singers declared that the visit had been one of the most interesting they had seen, and vowed that they would spread this knowledge wherever they found ears to listen.

And this they did for many a season.

OPPOSITION

We are back with the newly appointed Clan Chief Tiegn several generations later. The almost complete monument was now regularly used for Clan ceremonies and celebrations and to communicate with their ancestors when help was needed to resolve difficult issues. It had also become considerably more famous and visitors from lands far and near would arrive at any time. Unfortunately all too often they would arrive with little or no provisions and would expect to be looked after by the Clan, having been told that there was great wealth here. There had in fact been a few instances when stocks of grain were running low and such travellers had sadly been turned away leaving much ill feeling on both sides. It was Pandil the late Chief who had been made aware of regular thefts taking place at night and had set up a well armed squad who took it in turns to be the night watch and several would be thieves from other clans had been sent on their way disappointed and very hungry.

So it was that the great stone circle had a mixed reputation. Hated in some quarters, admired in others, but always respected even feared.

It was into this unstable situation that Vandil found himself set aside as his father's choice of Clan Chief, his sister—a woman—being

Tiegn and the Living Stones

appointed instead. True, his father had said that he would follow Tiegn—but by when? She was healthy and might even outlive him.

Tiegn was the child of his fathers first wife Nan who died shortly after Tiegn was born. Her father then took a second wife, Vandil's mother Jan, but their father in his heart was still in love with his number one Nan.

After Pandil had breathed his last, a very sore and angry Vandil went immediately to consult with his mother, for as he saw it she also had been slighted by his father's death-bed decision.

He found her sitting sunning herself on a straw bed outside their hut. She did not acknowledge him as he approached. He sat on a log by her side and for some time neither of them spoke. Not even a word of greeting.

Eventually Jan opened one eye and observed her son. She began mockingly—

'So, you have come to me for a bit of sympathy. Eh!'

Vandil was silent—this was too near the truth for comfort. After a pause she went on—'mmm. I know how you must feel, you have been by-passed, found not good enough, abandoned, discarded.'

Vandil reflected that this was exactly how he felt.

'But what I want to know is—just what are you going to do about it?' His mother asked.

'After all Tiegn is only a mere woman.' She cackled at this.

Tiegn and the Living Stones

The remark hurt Vandil—as it was intended to.

Neither spoke for some time.

'There are, I know, some of our Clan who hate the very idea of a female Chief. But would they support you or have they someone else in mind? Do you know?'

As she usually did his mother put her finger on the very aspect of the problem that was bothering him.

'No I don't,' he said.

'No,' said his mother, 'you don't.'

'However, I have been busy, and I have identified five or six of the senior men who want to see the Sword of Authority wielded by someone else.'

Vandil smiled at this.

'But don't get carried away—they may not want Tiegn as Chief—but they may not want you either,' she added.

This had occurred to Vandil—it was yet one more thing to consider.

But he ws now determined to depose Tiegn and to establish himself as Chief.

Tiegn and the Living Stones

The Dire Shape of An Aggressive Intent

The fame of the greatest stone circle was known to the occupied lands and was now universally accepted. Far from being the influence for good its builders had hoped it would be, it created strong feelings of envy and greed. There were more than one group seriously contemplating taking over the place by force, thus becoming the wealthiest people of all the surrounding territories.

It was one of the most notorious of these tribes that a disconsolate Vandil set out to find. His idea was to convince that tribe that when he was in control he would share the proceeds with them. His simple plan was to persuade a number of relatively dissatisfied men from Tiegn's Clan to combine forces with those of the clan he was visiting to create a combined assault group to march on the great circle. He knew Tiegn's Clan to be unarmed, and once there he would establish himself as the Clan Chief. He hoped, no—he intended that his dear sister would not survive the attack.

But first, he would like to know in advance just what the outcome of such aggression would be. He was forced to realise that such an adventure was not without its risks.

If anything his disappointment turned to anger with the passage of time.

Tiegn and the Living Stones

Thus it was some time after Tiegn's induction as Chief that Vandil took the first step. Thick cloud covered the sky, whilst a dull yellow half moon appeared from time to time, giving the surrounding woodland a timeless, wild feeling, like that of a wilderness. The soft grass hid Vandil's footsteps as he skirted the huts to avoid being seen. Arriving at one such hut standing on its own some distance from the rest he stopped at the entrance and called quietly. She appeared at the third call, and without any word of greeting vanished inside again clearly intending Vandil to follow. He entered the soft black void gingerly and waited for his eyes to become accustomed to the gloom challenged only by one small oil lamp.

Vandil found and sat on a bail of straw, and said nothing.

Salin the Seer sat opposite him and after they had both been silent for some time she said, 'So you decided, eventually, to call on an elderly woman with no man to provide for her.'

Vandil said nothing but emptied the contents of the sack he was carrying onto the straw covered floor, and out rolled several good apples.

'Yes that should be enough—so ask your question.'

Vandil hesitated, if the answer was 'no' he would be finished.

'Will you be clan Chief? You want to ask.' Salin put her finger directly on the reason for his visit.

'Yes,' he whispered.

Tiegn and the Living Stones

Salin nodded, but said nothing. She appeared to be listening.

After some time, it seemed much longer to Vandil, Salin nodded towards him and spoke in little over a whisper —

'The answer is 'Yes'' And she said no more for some time, occasionally waving Vandil to silence.

Vandil sensing that there was more to come did his best to wait quietly.

Then in an angry whisper, Salin said —

—'But you will live to regret it.'

A shocked Vandil jumped to his feet. 'What do you mean, tell me I insist . . . .'

'You can insist all you like,' Salin said quietly, 'but I have no more information — the ancestors have retired.'

Then in a normal tone — 'I am sorry but truly I have no more. The ancestors are now silent. They have spoken and they are most unhappy with what you intend, and they are definitely not on your side.'

Salin smiled at the now very angry Vandil and raised both her hands to try to placate him.

'You have not sought my council, but you shall have it anyway — I interpret what the ancestors have told me and I strongly urge that for yours and the Clan's well being you should give up your plan to be Chief. Take a wife and have a family instead — That is your route to happiness. But fool that you are — you will ignore this warning and will thus bringing pain to the scene instead of joy.'

A pause—then—

'That's all.'

At this Vandil very grudgingly thanked her, stood up, and found the entrance in the gloom. He tumbled out and as quietly as he could he left, sneaking, avoiding the paths. As he crept along he was accompanied by the noises of a woodland at night. Small animals scurried and squeaked as they made the most of the dark.

He had much to think about.

Salin's words were not to be ignored.

On the other hand she had been known to be wrong on more than one occasion. And she did say that he would be Chief and surely from that exalted position he aught to be able to control his destiny.

With this last thought in mind he decided to risk it—he would go ahead and grab for himself that which his father had denied him.

Ambition was now in full control, and he was sure that he would have his name in history. He would be sung about by the Story Singers wherever there were people to listen.

His next few days were full of preparations. The story he invented to disguise his intentions was that he knew nothing of the world outside the Clan and was bent on a trip of exploration.

But he fooled no-one.

It was some days later, the weather was wet and a damp mist hung about making mere shadows of the trees round about. Tiegn and Lakiln were seated alone in her hut discussing Vandils movements and decided they needed to know more. Lankiln had brought with him one who claimed friendship with Vandil but who was totally loyal to Tiegn.

'Well, what of Vandil's intentions then?' Lakiln asked him.

Denge considered for a moment, then said, 'You do know that he intends to take over the Clan and is at this very moment arranging to set out to obtain help in this endeavour.

'As far as I can tell—if he can gather a sufficiently motivated force he will try to overthrow you, and possibly murder you. How he intends to do this I don't know yet but when I do I will try to get a message to you. In the meantime I will go with him, fortunately I have done him one or two favours and he trusts me.'

Tiegn and Lakiln thanked him, and after checking that there was no-one about he left.

It pained Tiegn deeply that her brother, albeit half brother, would be prepared to kill her in order to establish himself as Chief. She considered resigning but heard her fathers words in her head. She would be Chief as he had ruled. She would need to find out who her friends were, and who were definitely enemies.

She held a get together deep in the woods, far from any prying eyes and was surprised and gratified that this small group had already set about preparing for hostilities and were totally loyal to her. The self appointed head of this group, Tensig, had discretely talked to most of the Clan and had ascertained that all but a very few supported Tiegn, and that most of the males would fight for her if it came to a show down. They discovered that not only was Vandil not to be trusted but was also generally disliked.

And so two secret armies were formed and discretely each began to obtain some kind of weaponry in order to be prepared in case it came to a fight.

Tiegn slept well that night.

Vandil made something of a show as he set out with five followers. They formed a small squad and marched out watched by just a few Clan members who could not stem their curiosity. The lack of obvious support angered him and he swore that he would stir things up when he was established as Chief.

Ten long days marching later he and a very hungry squad reached the home ground of the group he was heading for. If he was expecting a welcome of the kind any visitor to the Great Circle would have experienced he was disappointed. It was only when two heavily armed men accosted him and demanded to know what his business was, that he knew he was in the right place. He stated that he was there to see their Chief whose name he gathered was Roondot. But this was too easy and it was only after he had informed them where he was from that they agreed to escort him to the Chief.

Roondot stood head and shoulders above most of his clan and his physical strength was obvious from his taught muscles. He was known to have killed more than one of his enemies, of which he had plenty, without the aid of a weapon. He and his followers lived mostly by raiding nearby groups and taking everything they wanted.

It was this aggressive power that Vandil sought to help him achieve that which he desired above all else.

Roondot had a spy in Tiegn's clan and thus he already knew what Vandil was after, and he also knew the price that he would demand for his help.

The two met in the open where Roondot could see that Vandil and his men had only weapons of self defence. They sat on logs in a rough circle. Twenty-five or so of Roondot's men and Vandil's tiny troop of six. Roondot always saw to it that he had the numerical advantage, He also knew that the visitors were desperately hungry, and started by failing to offer them food.

Tiegn and the Living Stones

Roondot waved his men to silence, and waited. It was Vandil's call and Roondot was not prepared to help him.

And he continued to wait.

As Vandil was also silent, Roondot slowly rose and made to leave.

About to fail before he had begun Vandil blurted out—

'I am here to ask for help.' He said.

'Well what kind of help?' Roondot responded.

'I want a force strong enough to subdue those in charge of the Great Circle and see me made Clan Chief, just as my father should have done.'

'What of the opposition? Will they fight?' Roondot asked, although he already knew the answer.

'We expect they will put up an opposing force but it will only be small and totally inexperienced.' Vandil admitted.

'Still it will not be without its dangers, my people may get hurt, even killed—so what's in it for us?'

'There is an enormous cache of food to outlast the cold season—as Clan Chief I will allow you enough for all your requirements.'

'If you do that what will you and the clan survive on?'

'I will take all the workers in stone off their jobs and put them to finding food in the old way, by hunting, fishing and collecting fruit. We will manage.

'Will they obey you?'

Tiegn and the Living Stones

'They will with suitable threats from you.?' Vandil answered coldly.

At this point Roondot withdrew to one side and conferred with two of his men. After a short time he returned to Vandil.

'What you have offered is not enough.' He said. 'You are asking us to risk our lives for a few scraps of food. Surely you must see that it is not a fair exchange. I will do what you ask but in return you will appoint one of my men as your deputy, and five or six of them will join your inner circle.

Vandil was stunned, if he agreed Roondot would wield total control over the Clan.

'I can't do that,' he said angrily.

At this Roondot turned away, nodded to his men to follow and strode away, leaving Vandil and his troop alone and very hungry.

They pitched tents where they were.

Later after dark a woman who Vandil recognised as being related in some way to Salin sneaked into their camp with some food and drink—she left without a word.

The situation was discussed between Vandil and his men. He found that the men did not like Roondot's deal but felt that they had little choice. They offered a wavering support, not ideal Vandil thought—but all he could expect.

Morning arrived. Vandil had slept badly.

The day began with the woman of the night bringing some food—Vandil was shocked—The woman had clearly been beaten, she had deep bruising on her face and her left arm had been broken. She said that she was not allowed to speak to them and left without another word.

Life under Roondot would be rough—but he, Vandil, would be Clan Chief.

And so later that fateful day when they next met, under a clear blue sky, Vandil accepted Roondot's terms as that person knew that he would.

A few days later a strongly armed combined force under Roondot set off for the Great Circle.

It was depressingly wet when Roondot and his troop arrived at the Great Circle. For his men, it was their first sight of the enormous construction as they simply stood and gaped unable to grasp what it was the were looking at.

It was bigger by far than the biggest thing they had ever seen. It struck fear into every soul and one by one they dropped their weapons and knelt on the damp ground.

They were a tough bunch who had fought side by side with Roondot, but this was something else altogether. They were overwhelmed.

Just then, as they gaped, a rent in the clouds sent a dazzling shaft of light to strike the stones causing them to appear to glow as if they were on fire.

There were gasps from the group who were completely spellbound.

Roondot was the first to recover and cursed his men, but his words had little effect, the stones had impressed them with their power. That feeling of secret strength which was here

Tiegn and the Living Stones

displayed would for ever govern their deepest feelings. It was to prove to be a critical factor in the end.

With deliberate purpose, Roondot asked Vandil to take him to Tiegn.

Tiegn had been warned by the woman with the broken arm, who had run most of the way to warn them. Teign and Lakiln had had time to plan their strategy. With every appearance of welcoming them she offered the group hospitality and a hut to themselves. She told them that she would meet them the following day to discus their demands.

This seeming hospitality puzzled both Vandil and Roondot, and caused them to suffer a night of worry just as it had been designed to do.

Tiegn had realised that she must harness the power of the Great Circle and use it as a threat to gain some advantage. It was their only weapon but it held enormous power over minds which were unused to its overbearing presence.

She also had the foresight to have the Sword of Authority hidden and insisted she was not told of its resting place. She had made all the preparations she could — but would they be enough?

Dawn broke with a clear blue sky, and a smell of spring in the air. In the pre-dawn quiet Tiegn and her few helpers made their way quietly to the Great Circle and waited for the sun to break the horizon. As it did so they started the low chant that her father had taught her. Its haunting notes were heard by Roondot and his followers who slowly appeared to see what was happening, their curiosity winning over their apprehension. The scene which faced them they would never forget.

Tiegn and ten Clan's women dressed completely in white stood where the rays of the slowly rising sun bathed them as they sang. The song was of praise to the ancestors and thanks for their support in raising the stones to make this Great Circle. As the sun's orb cleared the horizon an equivalent squad of men also dressed in white appeared from the huts adding their voices to the song. As they strode to join the women the praise grew in volume and power eclipsing all other sounds and sending shock waves through the watching men.

Several fell to their knees trembling with fear.

Roondot appeared and shouted for silence, but his lone voice was drowned by the song and he understood for the first time just what he was up against. He realised that to act now would instantly put him in the wrong not only with the Clan but also with his own troop.

The power of the performance was felt even by him, deep in his soul he hesitated and wondered just what it was he might unleash. Nothing in his short life had prepared him for what he was witnessing.

But trembling with apprehension Roondot stood his ground until the chant eventually came to its conclusion with a massive shout that rent the morning air.

He tried to convince himself that ancestors or not, these people were only human with the

Tiegn and the Living Stones

usual human fears and ambitions, and he would deal with them as he had always done.

As the white clad singers retired from the scene, Roondot followed Tiegn and Vandil to the Chief's hut where Lakiln and a small core of senior Clans people were already waiting. Tiegn bid them sit and waited.

At length Roondot gathered himself and launched into his much rehearsed speech.

'I am greatly impressed by your great monument, for whatever purpose it was built I do not know. But what I do know its power can be used to subdue most of the surrounding Clans. It can make us all famous and powerful. So powerful in fact that we will be able to take whatever we need from whoever has it and we will never go hungry again.'

He paused and glared at the horrified Clans people.

'I intend to do this with the help of my men, so be prepared to accept this new force.'

And before anyone could object he went on—

'My first edict will be to replace Tiegn your present Chief with my own man namely young Vandil here.' At this he could not continue, his words being drowned as everyone wanted their say. When quiet was restored he did not wait to hear the objections but went on—'I have been told of the symbol of Clan power—the Sword of Authority so you will hand it over to me now please.'

At this, no-one moved or spoke.

Tiegn and the Living Stones

Eventually a very nervous Tiegn broke the silence—

'I am sorry but I have been told that it has been hidden and no one knows by whom or where.'

Roondat spoke quietly to a couple of his men who had just entered, and shortly after shouting and heavy blows could be heard outside.

Then two of Tingn's Clan each held from falling by two of Roodot's thugs staggered in and on being released fell to the floor—they had obviously been severely beaten judging by the blood seeping from open wounds. As they looked at Roondot they showed their hatred by the anger written on their faces. But they also carried a look of defiance and stubborn loyalty, a loyalty reserved for Tiegn and the clan.

Tiegn slowly turned a face to Roondot—'We cannot help you, they do not have the information. But I swear by the stones that you will pay for this.'

Roondot laughed—this was too easy. 'We do not need the sword,' he said 'Vandil is now Chief, and he will answer to me.'

However, the sword was so built into the Clan's beliefs that without it the Clan Chief's authority could belong to no-one, and this simple fact soon became key to the future. Vandil might declare himself Clan Chief but it was all self delusion, to the Clan without the sword he was just another ordinary Clansman. In fact, such was Roondot's impressive show of force that

Tiegn and the Living Stones

most of Teign's Clan did as they were told whilst Vandil was henceforth regarded as something of a joke, being referred to in private as Roondot's lap-dog

ROONDOT – A LOOSE SWORD

So who was this Roondot? How was it that he became the menace to the peaceful coexistence of the various clans in what was known as The Southern Realm of Kingdoms.

On the day of his birth his father, an aggressive individual, had picked a quarrel with the Clan Chief. He claimed that he should be second in the clan hierarchy in spite of the fact that he owed his existence to the Clan Chief's sister who had been raped whilst out in the woods on her own. In the short but brutal fight which followed Roondot's male parent was killed. In fact his demise was due to an accident. Taking a smart step backwards to avoid a blow from a heftily wielded axe, he tripped and fell backwards hitting his head on a standing stone as he fell. The blow did not kill him but the Clan Chief did.

His mother was overdue, and very underweight, close in fact to starvation. As a result he was lacking in weight at birth, and his mother only survived for a couple more days. Out in the, cold as it were, he was a survivor from the start. He found himself being brought up by anyone who had the time and food to spare. He learned the hard way how to scavenge and how to look as if nothing stood between him

Tiegn and the Living Stones

and starvation. It was a hard school with many a salutary lesson, and Roondot learned fast.

It was mostly either him or them and he made sure that it had to be him.

But on the whole the clan was good to him. There were those who took pity on the parentless child. And having received some trivial but unexpected kindness, he could also be very loyal.

He was noted for doing favours for those who assisted him. He effectively belonged to the whole Clan. As he grew, he developed a kind of honourable status almost on a par with the Chief. With such a bad start to life he was admired for the manner by which he survived. Even those who were reserved about him liked his resilience. As he grew to manhood his strength however lay in choosing his companions with great care. Thus ultimately power lay in the hands of a small group of dedicated followers. It became one of the ways that he survived that this group well armed would march out into no-man's land from where they would launch an attack on passing travellers or on small clan groups. They would steal anything worth the trouble, concentrating on foodstuffs. Eventually as more of the Clan realised the ease with which this could be achieved it became the way that their clan as a whole survived.

In all of this the Clan Chief took little part, being left out of most of the important decisions.

It is no longer known when the turning point was reached, but it was suddenly clear to everyone in the Clan that Roondot was playing

Tiegn and the Living Stones

the role of Chief. So much so that he was eventually accepted as the Chief. The natural successor to be Chief was only too happy to relinquish the position to a man who brought home such goodies. This way of life meant that Roondot was always on the lookout for easy pickings and his priority when not on the take was keeping his men up to their fighting best to be called upon at a moment's notice.

He had heard say about the Great Stone Circle, and recognised that it held special powers over men. Fear of this symbol of power was very much a part of the local folk law. Stories both false and true circulated whenever and wherever people met. It was believed by some that the stones had the power of life and of death which could be focussed on an individual or on a group. With some it was a taboo subject never to be mentioned for fear of its vindictive power. As with most outsiders this created a deep rooted fear, and for the most part Roondot was happy to leave well alone.

It was a policy which ensured his survival. Most of the other local groups learned to go about their lives whilst keeping a wary eye out for any of Ronndot's followers. If they had to travel they would do so in fairly large well armed groups.

Roondot ruled by fear. To offend him was to risk ones life. He remained un-loved and without a true friend. He became totally self reliant and foolishly brave. He was admired by some and hated by others.

Tiegn and the Living Stones

However, Roondot had recently recognised that his power was open to a challenge. The local groups had suffered at his hands just a little too often and rumour had it that they might be contemplating getting together to confront him.

And wary of the Great Circle Clan he kept his distance, but recognised that he might have to strike first.

Unfortunately the stones had their eyes on him.

Power Mis-used

Roondot decided that if he were to subdue the local groups he had to act speedily before they had chance to meet and form anything like an opposition.

So instead of consolidating his position with the Clan he persuaded Vandil to gather together all those of the Clan known to be prepared to join him with a view to making themselves rich in the process. Lakiln carefully inserted a man loyal to Tiegn into this force. He was to be key to the outcome.

His name was Betchen.

Then before another day had elapsed Salin, rarely seen outside her hut called on Tiegn. A storm was brewing as darkness took over the day. A powerful wind was toying with the trees, hiding any noise of passing feet. So quiet was she that a startled Tiegn was only aware of her presence when she had been standing there for some moments.

They were good friends who had shared their childhood and who trusted one another implicitly. Tiegn waved her hand as an invitation to Salin to be seated. Salin's silence conveyed her sympathy perfectly.

Eventually, Tiegn sighed and asked hesitantly 'What should I do?'

At this Salin looked sad, and replied, —'I am sorry, but I am not equipped to advise you as to which policy to pursue, but I have consulted the

Tiegn and the Living Stones

ancestors and I have come to reassure you as to the future outcome of these recent frictions.'

But instead of looking pleased Salin's face was a picture of despair.

Tiegn almost stopped her—she might be better off not knowing the future.

Salin understood, and allowed some time for Tign to prepare herself. Tiegn took the opportunity to pour a warming infusion into two cups which they sipped in silence for some time.

'Well then!' Tiegn said, and waited.

Salin began.

'Roondot will become powerful, There will be much fighting in which many in the Clan will suffer. The Clan will respect you for not leaving and saving yourself. Your half brother Vandil will side with Roondot and be given Chieftainship of the Clan.' She paused. 'Unfortunately that is all I can see.'

'Except,' she hesitated—'you will find a lover. There I have said too much.'

A clap of thunder drowned any further speech.

In the silence which followed Tiegn said—'Will I never again be Chief?'

'You must know that I have asked that question but I do not understand the answer.'

'Can you tell me what the ancestors said?' Tiegn asked.

'They said—"She, and only she, will know the answer." Was Salin's very short enigmatic reply.

'But I don't know.' Said Tiegn.

Salin regarded Tiegn in silence and finished her drink, after which they both stood and embraced warmly, and Salin left as unobtrusively as she had arrived.

She went unseen.

On a sun drenched day some time later the whole Clan was called to an enforced gathering in the shadow of the giant ring. Even those who were normally unable to walk were carried out protesting by those who had decide to join Roondot's force. Roondot had ensured that these men were crudely armed.

Roondot's tiny force was pathetically small as they faced the bulk of the Clan which was spread out around his troop. Nevertheless the military aspect of the men created fear amongst the Clan—just as they were intended to do.

When the last straggler had arrived, Roondot stood on a large stone which was originally destined to become one of the bridging lintels. He then assumed his fiercest aspect and with a grim face he waved his hand for silence, and very quickly all conversation died out.

'Members of the Clan,' he began, 'you now have a new Chief.' He raised both arms to quell the noise that this announcement created. 'Your Chief from today is someone you all know well. Vandil here is now that man. He has my full backing and any opposition will be referred to me, and this will result in severe punishment.'

This statement was greeted by a low growling sound of resentment from the Clan. If anyone

Tiegn and the Living Stones

was pleased at this announcement they didn't show it.

Roondot waited for the clamour to die down, and then spelled out a few of his rules:—

'From now on there will be a change to what you will be asked to do—for a start, completion of the last secion of the stone circles will be given a low priority. Work of this nature will only be allowed when there is little or no other activities in hand.' He paused to let this is sink in.

'Next—consulting the ancestors except at my or Vandil's request from now on is strictly forbidden.'

He was interrupted by a louder groan from his audience.

'Please do not fret I aim to use the power of the stones to make us all very rich—we will never go without food again.'

This was greeted by applause from his troop and silence from the Clan who did not believe what they were being told.

'That is all for now. Please return to what you were doing and await further instructions which will be announced by Vandil.

He waved his hand and a disgruntled, grumbling Clan slowly drifted back to the huts.

It was the beginning of what became known as The Bad Times.

Roondot needed to stamp his policy on the Clan. He sent out men to gather information about the nearby Clans mostly as to their vulnerability.

He gathered his force together as a raiding party. And after ensuring that Vandil was left fully in charge of the Clan, moved into the woods to train his troop.

The Clan did their level best to carry on in the manner to which they were accustomed. The stone workers carried on preparing the next big stone to be added to the circle but were forcibly stopped by Vandil and a couple of Roondot's men. They were then instructed to collect something to be used as a weapon and to join Roondot's force.

They complied but with some show of reluctance, but one of their number was beaten as an example to any others who might choose to ignore Roondot's rules.

It became clear to both Vandil and to Roondot that although these co-opted troops did as they were instructed, should they be required to fight side by side with Roondot's men their loyalty could not be relied upon and many would in all likely-hood change sides.

Roondot's rule had its limits.

Eventually both Vandil and Roondot came to realise that issuing edicts was one thing but asking peace loving people to take up arms against people whom they had previously regarded as friends was a quite different proposition.

Several of Tiegn's loyal men refused to comply with the new rules. They were willing to risk "severe punishment" rather than carrying out acts which were against their established beliefs. It was not the way in Tiegn's Clan.

The atmosphere was tense and unhappy and —
Something had to give.

AN INTERLUDE

Into this scene of trouble just waiting to be unleashed came a visit from a pair of Story Singers.

Their appearance on the scene was reported to Vandil who decided that they should be treated as normal and provided them with a hut, It was suggested to them that he would be pleased to see them after they had eaten. They stood as he entered and he waved them to be seated.

'You are welcome here as usual.' He said. 'Perhaps you will join us this evening, and tell us the news. In the meantime you are free to wander anywhere you like and talk to anyone. I only ask that you see me before you leave and tell me what you have learned.'

The Story Singers thanked him for his courtesy, ... 'we will be there.' They said.

It was a fine clear night with a cold full moon splashing the Giant Ring with pale light. The sky was wreathed with tiny bright sources of light some of which had names. All who could be there—were there, huddled round the warming glow of the log fire.

When he judged that the last person had arrived the senior singer stood and announced their first contribution.

'Thank you all for your most generous welcome.'

Tiegn and the Living Stones

'We would like to begin with a song of what is happening beyond your boundaries. Beware it is not a happy tale. But we will sing it as it is.

They began in harmony—

> Where there once was peace,
> And the many Clans were friends,
> Now talk of war will never cease,
> And aggression never ends.
>
> A new feeling goes abroad,
> Wherever one may stray,
> Everyone waves his sword.
> Someone will have to pay.

This song was greeted by a meager clapping from a couple of Roondot's men.

The singers then embarked on a couple of equally gloomy songs which painted a picture of pending hostilities.

It was too much for some, and a few began to drift quietly away. The singer's reputation as entertainers was now at risk and so they began several verses of a more humorous tone.

> We were at the clan of the Giant Stone Ring,
> And one stone was ready to lift,
> It lay there as a dead thing,
> But the men stood ready to shift.
> The stone had to be lifted to be put in its place,
> The gang boss was all ready to go.

Tiegn and the Living Stones

> And up went the stone swift as a dart,
> In place—but trapping his toe.
> To try and get free he put up a fight,
> But sad to relate he was there all the night.
> They dug a hole right under his foot,
> And freed his leg now a horrible sight,
> Now he shouts his instructions from the door of his hut.

This was more like it. The applause lasted a long time, after which they finished with a couple of nursery songs for the children who were allowed up late as a treat.

It was clear to anyone who had witnessed the visit that the Singers were not happy with the atmosphere of the place. Early the following day they left. Their experience would be news and a warning to the nearby groups.

Tiegn and the Living Stones

A Growing Up

The work on the stones was the most important activity that the Clan had ever undertaken. They considered that it was in fact the main reason for their existence. The plan for the way Double ring was to look when complete had been handed down through the many generations that had given all their time to its creation. Many had spent their whole lives on its construction. Now at long last it was approaching completion. Thus, the present workers could see what a magnificent and impressive sight it was. And now as each new day arrived the rings stood there as a great symbol of the clan's achievement and the driving force in their lives. They could not conceive of a life without the need for work on the stones.

The Story Singers told them that there was nothing to compare with the Great Stone Circle even across the big waters.

One of these workers in stone—Sentin, had spent all of his long life shaping the giant stones so that each one could take its part in the final structure. He had trained his son Wellin in the stone mason's craft and they had worked side by side chiselling the stone day in day out throughout their lives, with great patience. They were skilled in the techniques required to shape the stone. And skilled they were, but this was their only skill, they knew nothing of other work.

In order to concentrate on the job their meals and drinks were brought to them each day by

Tiegn and the Living Stones

their women folk. Just where this tasty daily fare came from they only had a vague idea. Sentin was a typical shaper of stone who relied on his life-long partner Shelly to provided their sustenance. However he did know that her work was at times as strenuous as his. He was also aware that her activities were as weather dependent as were his. It was a hard existence but it was also satisfying especially now as the ring was approaching its final shape. The thing was nearly finished.

As well as the work, they had a son and a daughter between them, the son was twelve years old and the other fifteen. Naturally the girl spent her day with their mother. Life for the youngsters could be harsh. The women's lives consisted of an almost endless struggle to provide enough food for themselves and the men. Even in good times and during the warm season they would have precious little time for themselves.

The Clan's year was split roughly into four parts equal in length. It would begin in the later of the two warm periods when they would harvest the crops of fruit and gather the seed, and if the weather had been favourable there would be plenty, and life would be easier.

Later as the weather got colder the ground had to be prepared and the seed had to be planted. This was hard work, and their hours were long. They would often be working after sunset, and sometimes even by the light of a full moon in cloud free sky.

Tiegn and the Living Stones

It always seemed that there was never enough time for the family to enjoy with each other.

In inclement conditions crude canopies of leafy branches could be erected over the stone being worked on. The work of knocking chunks off the stone with tools of deer antler bone, flint, or exceptionally much treasured bronze would continue.

A woman was old at thirty seasons, and a man five seasons later, and most of their time was spent with the rest of the Clan and working.

Regular and un-scheduled meetings were held at the stone circles to resolve Clan issues and to communicate with their ancestors. These were usually presided over by The Clan Chief or his deputy.

Knowledge of what was going on outside the Clan's nominal boundary was provided by the occasional visits from the Story Singers who as they travelled turned into song all the news they had picked up. Such visits were always much appreciated.

Shell, Sentin's daughter had reached that place in her life when she was aware of basics of life having assisted at the birth of several of her mothers closer friends. She had also experimented superficially with the sexual aspect of life, but so far had felt little affection for those to whom she had permitted small favours.

Tiegn and the Living Stones

She as pure blonde and by any standards immensely attractive being full of the joy of life with a cheerful disposition. Shell was also that much sort after female in that she was considered a hard worker, always taking her share of whatever work needed doing. In addition she had one interesting quality which was not very common, and that is—she had a deep appreciation of the way things looked, she had in fact an artistic flair. For example—not being satisfied with the way something appeared she would seek to change whatever aspect she found that could be improved. Theirs was the only dwelling with flowers growing around it.

Shell was also growing restless.

Then one warm night when sleep was denied her she took a stroll through the trees, her footsteps aided by a very full moon. As she walked she became aware of a feeling in her body which she had never before experienced, a strange feeling of urgency. She felt as if something important and which she desperately needed was missing.

Then, turning a corner in the path she heard the unmistakable sound of human voices, talking quietly.

And then quite suddenly in a grassy glade there they were—her brother and a girl.

The obvious thing was that they were both naked, their bodies white in the moonlight.

The boy was lying on his back and was moaning quietly. The girl was astride him moving against him rhythmically her full

Tiegn and the Living Stones

breasts stroking his chest. Shell could see that her eyes were closed and her face showed deep concentration. Shell felt a stirring in her own young frame and her hand reached down and she let her fingers gently stroke herself.

The couple were still engaged in their activity as Shell left the glen. She felt alive with an urging that she had previously never experienced. A strong physical thrill coursed through her body. Something very fundamental had changed and she knew that she could never no go back.

Some instinct told her that she had ceased to be a girl and had become a woman. And there in the woods now all on her own she laughed out loud just for the joy of it.

Back in the glade the couple were so engrossed in each other that they never heard her.

She wondered vaguely if the feelings she felt would vanish with the dawn like so many of the night things did. But deep in her physical being she knew that the changes she felt would stay and eventually become a driving force in her life.

In the light of dawn on the following morning she had a clear physical indication that womanhood had arrived. She knew from overheard discussion between the women folk that it was considered good manners to stay way from contact with the men and boys.

On that first day Shell's mother sensing what had happened, relieved her of any tasks suggesting instead that she took a short walk and relaxed in the warm mid-year sunshine.

Tiegn and the Living Stones

As Shell lay dreaming on a grassy bank she could see men working, and wondered what taking a man was like. A part of her was nervous of the experience whilst she also felt a great desire to try it.

Then a shock.

If she was to do this thing—with whom would it be? So far she had felt only friendliness for her male acquaintances. She went through them in her mind and decided that there was no-one amongst the young fellows whom she liked well enough to share her new feelings.

She smiled to herself—it really was something to look forward to.

Some Rivers Run Deep

It was generally understood that Tiegn was promised to Betchen. Nothing was announced, nothing formal that is. But it would be hard to find anyone in the Clan who did not know of their association. Any observant individual seeing the way they treated each other even the way they looked at each other would immediately understand.

Why they had not made this formal lay in the tremendously busy life they both led.

For both of them the day started at sunrise which signalled to Tiegn that she was due to visit the stones for the start of day communication with the ancestors.

This consisted of a visit to the stones where she would kneel and relate the previous day's activities, followed by the plan for the coming day and asking for their help if it were needed.

About now Deputy Lakiln would appear and Tiegn would first listen to any problem he might have then she would advise him of her plan for the day. He then usually thanked her and retired to get the work underway.

On her return she would wander about the group of huts, the Clan's living quarters, to get a feel for the mood — was it one of light hearted constructive activities with frequent well wishers waving to her. Or was it a miserable wet day with everyone finding jobs indoors and a bucket full of problems for her to try and resolve.

Tiegn and the Living Stones

On her daily round she always called on any sick or on anyone in the process of giving birth or carrying a child.

She was well liked, and having got over the fact that their Chief was a woman they gave her the respect that was due to a Clan Chief.

But Tiegn's feeling for Betchen was not the only romantic tale that was part of the Clan's gossip, Stentin was becoming increasingly concerned for his daughter Shell.

When Roodot's men were wandering about the surrounding territories one or two stayed preferring that way of life, much to Roondot's annoyance.

One of these, a young man called Style, took to building himself a hut on the edge of The Clans territory on a piece of land which butted up to Stentin's place.

It was inevitable that he and Shell should meet and even spend some time together.

Unfortunately the lad was still loyal to Roondot.

Shell soon fell to admiring Style's firm young frame, and her dreams of him were mixed up with memories of what she had witnessed in the woods.

Her new feeling of womanhood was stirring deep in her body.

It was on one of those oppressively hot days which were no cooler when the sun went down below the horizon but left behind a sky that gave enough light to be able to see as if it was day. Style had spent his time admiring the work

Tiegn and the Living Stones

of the stone masons. He was fascinated to see a neatly shaped stone with regular corners and a beautifully smooth face immerge from the crude lump that arrived at the mason's yard. He decided that if he were allowed to join the Clan he would become a stone worker. But would they let him? Then he had an idea. They might if he were associated with one of the females from the Clan.

As this idea claimed his objective he remembered seeing the girl Shell and all of a sudden a plan emerged.

And so on this very warm day Style sought out Shell whom he found busy washing some garments in a small pool cut into the bank of the river and made for that purpose. He needed an excuse to be there, so he speedily made his way back to his hut and returned with his fishing equipment, and some bait.

The place he chose to fish from was on the bank well within talking distance from Shell.

He quickly realised that he had no idea how to engage her in conversation, he had little or no experience to help him.

But as with some cases it all happened naturally.

He landed a fish, and a good sized fish it was.

And then a second and two more.

Satisfied he had enough fish. He planned to keep two and offer two to Shell.

He looked at the cool water flowing gently past and after a battle with his conscience removed his clothing apart from his lower

Tiegn and the Living Stones

covering to preserve some dignity. And then he gingerly slid down the bank and into the wonderful refreshing swirl of the river. Fortunately it was not very deep here, only waist high, and slow moving, so the fact of his not being able to swim was not important. He so enjoyed his dip that his intentions towards Shell was momentarily forgotten.

This state of affairs could not last for long.

Quite suddenly a completely naked woman was splashing towards him. Her enjoyment of the river brought a happy smile to her face. Only a hand's reach away she stood up and grinned at him, and he knew two things at the same time which threatened to overwhelm him. One—that he had never seen anything quite so lovely,—and two—that they would make love.

They laughed and splashed one another and he found himself without his lower garment.

Now it was that Shell could see quite clearly the effect that she was having and was glad. Their splashing became a kind of friendly wrestling.

Then suddenly whilst still in the river she felt him inside her, but before she could enjoy the sensation it was all over.

Then to Style' surprise Shell then proceeded to wash him down as if he were part of her washing basket her hands caressing his manhood. After which they climbed out and lay quietly side by side on the grassy bank their bodies just touching here and there. She sighed as his hands strayed over her breasts and as she

Tiegn and the Living Stones

was again aroused they made love slowly and for sometime. Until in fact exhaustion overtook their desires.

And so they became lovers and began to make plans to tell Shell's father and for her to share Style's hut and seek the formal blessing of the Chief to recognise that their relationship was permanent.

Tiegn and the Living Stones

Reaction

In time word of the association of Style with what he regarded as an enemy reached Roondot. That person regarded this liaison as a betrayal of his intentions to take over one or more of the smaller outlying groups by force. If that kind of thing became general his long term plans would be undermined. He therefore determined that the liason should be destroyed.

With this evil in mind he sent for two of his trusted henchmen. These two Pern and Thengis had been recipients of masses of wealth captured by Roondot. They owed him for their current opulent lifestyle.

At their briefing meeting, Roondot laid out his plan for them to follow.

'It is vital,' he began,'—that no one suspects that we are actively behind the break up of this foul relationship, so I suggest that you tackle the problem in three distinct phases.'

His two henchmen both felt unhappy with the task he had charged them with. This was most definitely not the kind of thing that they had signed on for. But they had little choice.

'Firstly, you must try to lure the lad back onto our side with promises of great wealth and recognition of a job well done.

'Secondly—If number one fails you must try to lure the girl away from the lad even if she finds him with one of you.

'Thirdly—If all else does not work—you will lure the lad away and make him understand that his very life depends on it. If that doesn't have the right effect then you have no alternative but to kill him. We will use his death as a message to anyone else who is planning to change sides. Is that all clear to you both?'

The two unhappy men nodded silently. And left looking and feeling most desperately concerned.

They knew that if they failed then it would be their lives which would be sacrificed. And their real problem was that they really did not trust each other.

But nevertheless they prepared themselves and two very nervous souls headed out to Stentin's small Clan.

They did however eventually manage to get to meet their target reminding him of his background. This was just what Style did not want to hear, and would make himself scarce when he saw the two appear.

They even managed to convince him that a big fat reward awaited him if he would come back with them to the clan. But when he discussed this with Shell he found that he would have to go alone. She would have no part in it. Roondot's reputation was against him.

So the two men moved on to try Roondot's step two, fearful as they were of bringing his wroth down on themselves if they failed.

Tiegn and the Living Stones

Loyalty Betrayed

As sometimes happens in life, actions of a seemingly trivial nature have an unexpected, and occasionally, cataclysmic effect which can be way beyond original intention. It's as if a man were to sneeze and thus bring down a whole mountain swallowing a city on its slopes.

The two Roondot's men tried to worm their way un-noticed into Stentin's Clan. which was like poking a wild boar with a stick. For a start they stood out like flowers in a desert. They wore Roondot's gifts which were out of place amongst that poor but thrifty group of hard working peoples. They also had goods enough to trade for a hut instead of having to build their own.

And they were never seen to do any actual work. The Clan did not know why they were there, regarding them with suspicion.

From then on, almost every day Style was to be found assisting Shell in whatever task she was engaged in. He began to understand how the Clan worked and he started to appreciate how they were able to find the time and the manpower to raise those massive hunks or solid rock. This was not easy for a man who had been raised in a quite different regime, but he managed it. And not only did he do so but found that he could actually bring the odd new idea to the team.

Roondot's men were about to embark on part two of the strategy, that is to try to lure

Shell away from her loved one. Since Shell was an attractive proposition anyway they almost came to blows between each other as to who should be the one to try. In the end they pulled straws. Pern won and set out to try but Shell found his bumbling attempts at seduction were so nauseating that she complained to Style. Style complained to the Chief. Chief Stentin was so angered by this interference with his people that he issued a open threat to Roondot that he would personally see to it that Roondot's life would be forfeit. And he sent the pair back to Roondot with this message.

Roondot was so incensed that he decided that this clan should be the first to be attacked.

WAR

Roondot was now ready to put his plan into action. His force had been training in the nearby woods for some time. They had been observed and their activities had been reported to Tiegn.

Then came that evil day.

The weather was dry but with a very cold breeze making furs essential and the group of men of which only a small number were recruited from Tiegn's Clan were eager to get moving.

Roondot had left Vandil in sole charge of Tiegn's Clan and Vandil began to show his authority from the very start.

Early on the day following Roodot's march Vandil called on all the male Clan members to meet him in the centre of the ring of stones.

There was much puzzled discussion as to what it was all about — they were soon to find out and it was not a happy occasion.

Vandil stood on a stone which raised him above the crowd.

He did not waste any time on preliminaries, but weighed straight in —

'Right,' he said, 'As the only male child of my father I believe that it is I and only I who should inherit the Chieftainship of this Clan. So as Chief I intend to make some drastic changes. Therefore I have decided on some new rules —

Tiegn and the Living Stones

'Firstly—Using the Stone Circles as a means to contact the ancestors is forbidden from now on—anyone discovered to be trying to do this will be severely punished. I will be the only person to talk to them and pass on to you what they say.'

This statement was greeted by loud boos and angry comments from the group. Eventually the noise was subdued as Roodots men left behind to support Vandil, stepped forward aggressively.

'Next—,' he said when the noise had died down—'I am now in charge of this Clan and my decisions will be promptly obeyed.'

This was greeted by a stony silence. Anger was mounting in the crowd.

'In any dispute about food distribution I will decide and my decision will be final.'

'Anyone seen wandering about after sunset will also be severely dealt with.'

Also I have decided that we have spent too much time preparing and raising the great stones, so half the men still engaged in this work will be asked to cease and find other employment.

This raised an angry and continuous roar from the clansmen.

Vandil tried to quieten them but failed.

In a vain attempt to show that he was still in charge he shouted a single word—

'Dismiss.' But it had no effect.

Vandil turned away and gradually, finding themselves without a target for their anger they quietened down somewhat.

Tiegn and the Living Stones

Vandil then tried to press on with a couple more minor rules but failed.

He waved a hand to indicate the meeting was at an end, and they were to disperse.

A disconsolate group of Clan members grumblingly drifted off.

And so were the seeds of trouble planted.

—It did not take long to bear fruit.

When Tiegn heard what had taken place she found it hard to believe that Vandil would attempt to usurp her authority in this manner. She thought that he must be loosing his grip on reality. She wondered if the Clans folk would obey him. Perhaps some might, but not all of them she thought. She resolved not to let her grip on authority slip from her grasp.

She sent Lakiln to find Vandil and bring him to her so that she could confront him. Lankiln reported hat he was not to be found.

A day or two later Tiegn was in her hut discussing issues with Lakiln when Vandil burst in pushing a man in front of him and they were quickly followed by Denge, Vandil's newly appointed deputy, and Tiegn's spy.

Once inside Vandil forced the man to kneel, and as he looked up Tiegn recognised him as Tensig a man of integrity and one of her true followers.

'This man is a traitor.' Shouted Vandil. 'He was caught trying to talk to the ancestors which is strictly forbidden and he deserves severe punishment as an example to others, and as you no longer have any authority here I intend to have him whipped in front of the Clan.'

He grasped the man by his ear and forcing him to his feet turned to leave the hut.

'Just one moment please.' Said Tiegn firmly. And so used to taking orders instead of giving them, Vandil hesitated in the doorway.

'Allow me to remind you of a few facts. You were appointed Chief by Roondot, but he is not even a Clan member and so I for one do not recognise his or your authority here. There has been only one person named by the long standing rules of the Clan and by the previous Chief—and that person was me. Therefore the truth is that I and not you or anyone else is the rightful governing authority here.'

She paused to let this sink in.

Vandil stood still, he had never seen his half sister take such a formidable stand.

Tiegn continued—'I still have the ear of the ancestors and I can tell you that they also do not accept your authority. So—If I were you I would take a good look around and note that you are well outnumbered here and your life will be worth nothing should you harm this man.'

Vandil paled as he recognised the truth of her words, but he had laid down the law in public and therefore had to go ahead with his intention or be sidelined by all those who were with Tiegn.

'We shall see.' He roared as he shoved his prisoner out and followed him.

Tiegn and the Living Stones

The following day was bleak and cold with a pale sun shining through a thin mist, when Vandil called for the Clan to meet at the entrance to the outer Circle and to be there when the sun had reached its highest point.

As they assembled, grumbling at being taken from their work, they saw that Tensig was standing tied to one of the giant upright stones naked to his waist.

Standing to one side of him stood one of Roondot's men casually swishing a rope whip.

Behind this tableau stood the three men that Roondot had left to support Vandil.

Nothing like this had ever happened before and a shocked Clan stood and gaped.

Vandil siezed the moment.

Shouting above the rumble of voices he began—

'This man has defied my strict rule about consulting the ancestors. He knew well enough that what he was doing and that he was breaking my ruling.

He stopped in the silence which followed. Then—

'I have decided therefore that I have no other choice than that he shall be punished.'

He hesitated as Tiegn's sudden appearance was greeted by a low cheer from the clan.

But now Vandil was committed.

'This wrong doer will have twelve lashes for his misdeeds.'

Tiegn and the Living Stones

'Stop.' Shouted Tiegn, 'If you proceed with this I will order the Clan to deal with you in the same manner.

Vandil hesitated as this was greeted with a loud cheer from the Clan, and crude weapons began to appear amongst them.

Roondot's men looked nervous, their position was beginning to look precarious.

Vandil turned to the man with the whip—'Twelve lashes NOW.' He ordered.

Roondot's men stood no chance as a horde of men of the Clan surged forward and with a great shout quickly overwhelming them.

Tensig was cut free. And one by one, including Vandil, Roondot's men, had their hands tied and were led away.

Before the crowd dispersed Lakiln shouted over the clamour for quiet and in the silence Tiegn ordered the wrong doers to be held as prisoners and she would declare their future tomorrow. She left the scene to a great cheer.

These were shaping up to be the very worst of the the Bad Times.

———◆•◆•◆———

As luck would have it the day following the debacle the rain came down heavily and few were about.

Tiegn called on Lakiln, and having considered the matter overnight wanted to get his approval for her actions.

Tiegn and the Living Stones

'Well.' She said when they were comfortably seated. 'This is what I want to do. These men when they act as a group are not only a danger to us but they consume precious stores. I therefore intend to try and split them up. With the exception of Vandil, and starting tomorrow we will release them one at a time every two days. My guess is that most of them finding themselves alone will make their way back home. So what do you think?'

Lakiln was truly impressed by Tiegn's strategy, and promptly gave his OK. 'I will start to make preparations now,' he said.

When the news of this got around it was clear that it met with approval.

The only problem remaining was what to do with Vandil. For the time being he was allowed to go anywhere he chose but always shadowed by a guard. It was only a matter of time before he escaped, as Tiegn anticipated, and made his way to where Roondot and his troop were camped.

Roondot was displeased with Vandil as news of the debacle had reached him.

He gave instructions that if Vandil appeared he was to be and brought straight to him to answer for his failings.

A dishevelled, tired, and defeated Vandil was brought directly to Roondot's tent. Vandil knew he had failed but blamed it on Roondot for not providing enough men.

Roondot let him stand as a few of his force sat to watch the proceedings.

It proved to be very short.

Tiegn and the Living Stones

Roondot—'So, I left you in charge and now you are here.'

Vandil—'Yes, but we were outnumbered.'

Roondot—'But you let this happen.'

Vandil—'I was let down, betrayed.'

Roondot—'By whom?'

Vandil—'By those I trusted.'

Roondot—'The failure then was yours. For trusting those you guessed were not with you.'

Vandil—gave a grudging nod.

'I have heard enough,' said Roondot. 'You still need to prove yourself worthy of my friendship and support. Now please get out of my sight—I will decide what to do with you in due course.'

Vandil had the sense to keep his deep feeling of injustice to himself, he felt strongly that his time was yet come. Roondot had made a dedicated enemy.

A day or two passed and Roondot realised that if he delayed much longer his men, who were already wondering why they were there, would begin to drift away. Two had already gone. He therefore determined that the nearest camp would be his first target. However the weather was still bad and the attack was postponed.

It was now that those two Story Singers stumbled on Roondot's camp. Roondot thought that their songs would improve morale and made them welcome.

Tiegn and the Living Stones

The following evening ending a day of warm sunshine they sang to the group and were rewarded with enough food for several days. But they also had time to talk to the men and were told of the impending attack.

Roondot suspected this, but felt that as the target group was one of the new style settled ones, they would have nowhere to escape to. He also hoped that any news would be likely to create an atmosphere of fear.

The Story Singers arrived at the targeted group to be very warmly received. They were however wary of their passing on of information and asked for a day of rest, It was a couple of days later when good fire was crackling away as the group prepared to do justice to the event. Everyone who could be there was there.

Roondot's spies were present and watchful.

The singers arrived and were greeted with warm applause. And after they had eaten, they began with a new song in praise of the sun which they said had several meanings. It was only short and the meaning behind the words was very clear.

> A great red orb graces the day,
> And helps the plants to grow,
> Its warmth will chase the frost away,
> But beware of the hungry crow.
>
> These birds will come at night,
> Creeping in without a sound,

> And so without a fight,
> They spread their wings around.

The true meaning of these words was not wasted on the group who now knew how and when Roondot would attack. Strangely but perhaps because his spies had been plied with drink laced with a juice that made one dizzy, they missed the message. They also cheered the loudest.

At the end of the evening and several songs later the Singers retired some distance away from the scene. By the dawn they had gone.

It was Roondot's plan to attack at dawn. During the night his men would sneak in under cover of darkness and surround the camp. Then at the first light of day would rush the group taking them completely by surprise.

Knowing this the group's leader just as dusk was descending had everyone move out and hide themselves with their makeshift weapons some distance from the huts. Here and there an oil lamp was lit in the huts to give the place an occupied appearance.

And into the trap sneaked Roondot's unsuspecting men. Roondot himself was some distance away and ready to walk in to a newly captured clan. And so the two forces waited uncomfortably for the first rays of the morning sun.

As an army Roondot's men were inferior in number but were better armed.

So what of the outcome?

Tiegn and the Living Stones

The result was forgone.

Roodot's men stood and charged, but unfortunately for them they mis-timed it and did not all move together.

So the defenders were able to subdue Roondot's force fairly easily as they leaped out of the undergrowth in twos and threes.

It was all over as the sun climbed higher. Roondot's men were all captured whilst he and Vandil managed to slip through the net and escape.

But neither were about to give up. There were other ways.

AN AMUSING INTERLUDE

A series of warmer days followed during which work returned to normal. The final stones were being worked on, and huts and farming tools repaired. It was during this lull that a famous incident occurred which was eventually captured in song by the Story Singers.

Some time back a very old woman with many disabilities surprised everyone by giving birth to a son. The lad was much bigger than others of his age with a natural strength and found useful employment helping the stone shapers to move the more manageable blocks of stone.

One day a hunting group brought back from an expedition not only a couple of good sized boars killed by well aimed spears, but they also had a small male boar still very much alive. Not knowing just what to do with this animal, it was given to Reb, as this lad was named, to look after until it was big enough to be eaten.

Now the animal grew very large and powerful, a fair match for Reb, and they went everywhere together, it followed him happily on a rope lead.

He named the thing Bork which was old name for a boar, and he even spent a great deal

Tiegn and the Living Stones

of time trying to teach the animal to talk. He often got his leg pulled.

'Your Bork told me a real tale about you and the girls, you lucky lad.' They might say, 'You should tell him to keep those things to himself.'

But on one of those light evenings as the Clan was enjoying a well earned communal get together our Reb appeared with his boar in tow. He was always popular and it was that one of the Clan was teasing the lad. 'By! But that animal is getting too big for you lad, I bet you could almost ride him.' This was greeted by much laughter and cheering. Our Reb stood and looked at the animal and you could see the words gathering into action in his head.

Then with no more ado he flung a leg over the boar and sat firmly upright on its back with a huge grin on his face. He held on by grasping the hairs on the back of the animal. The crowd went wild, and cheered loudly.

Now the boar was used to being led around but was not at all happy with the full weight of Reb on his back. It spun around two or three times but failed to dislodge its rider who hung on grimly. It was now quite angry and then suddenly the animal with its rider took off at great speed dashing between the huts scattering people on either side. The crowd were very much enjoying this unexpected entertainment and followed in pursuit, cheering and shouting encouragement as they ran.

'Hang on there Reb, you will tame him yet.'

It became something of a game as the boar charged about between the huts scattering the watchers to left and right as it went with the lad still clinging to its back.

The crowd went wild.

'Go it Reb'

'Ride him lad — I do believe your faster than a horse.'

In and out of the huts they hurtled, swerving, and doubling back with the boar trying to dislodge the boy still holding on as if his life depended on it.

For some time the pair were inseparable — but then the boar got too close to the river, and as it turned to avoid it, the animal skidded and tumbled down the bank throwing Reb in a graceful arc into the middle where he entered the water with a great splash to be followed by the boar.

It was then realised that although the lad was unable to swim and was about to drown, the boar was a natural swimmer and was making good progress to the opposite bank.

Several pairs of hands made a chain and helped Reb to the side where they all climbed out. They were just in time to see backside of the boar as it disappeared into the trees, still going at top speed now without the weight of its rider — it was never seen again.

That evening round the communal fire Reb was accorded a hero's reception.

And as was mentioned the event was in due course captured in song by the Story Singers.

THE STRUGGLE GOES ON

Roondot had suffered something of an ignominious defeat. Not only that but his troops were scattered and most had gone into hiding being concerned about reprisals. And for some considerable time a kind of wary peace settled upon the groups of settlers around the Great Stone Circles. Roondot kept a low profile, licked his wounds and made plans. His ambition had not waned in the slightest, he was still determined to capture that Great Ring of Stones and use their inherent power to make himself something of a king figure reigning over all the local settlements, as a kind of benevolent dictator.

To this end he sent his two best men out to explore the surrounding groups and to report back to him on their strengths and weaknesses. Back at his base he had built a larger than usual hut on the floor of which he caused to be laid a good thick layer of sand. By scribing grooves in the sand with a stick he made a good enough resemblance to the actual world around him but on a manageable scale He furnished it with a collection of lots of coloured stones which he sited to represent the other living groups. It was an early forerunner of our modern day accurate maps.

Tiegn and the Living Stones

As his scouts returned they would retire to this ground plan to refine it by adding their new information a bit more each time. It became easy to see where the strengths lay and more especially the weaknesses. Roondot tried to keep this model secret, but it was impossible to hide such a unique piece of work.

Knowledge of it filtered out and acted as a warning to the nearby peoples that trouble in the shape of Roondot was not far away. The more sensible of them developed a rota of sentries to give warning of aggression. They also met and agreed strategies to be employed if attacked.

Roondot had wanted to ensure that the next time he set out to grab the land occupied by the local groups, the result would be very different from last time, but news of his intentions was abroad.

At the Great Stone Circle, Vandil had no such ambitions, he merely wanted to take his rightful place at the head of his father's Clan. He felt that he still had one or two friends back in his Clan, and sneaked back under cover of darkness to contact them. Bendin was a disgruntled stone worker. His work on the stones was often declared of a poor standard and had to be re-done. His workmanship often provoked laughter leaving him angry and frustrated. He was just the sort that Vandil wanted to recruit to his cause. And so began a new phase in the battle for absolute control of the Clan.

It was on a warm sunny day around the time the Clan planted the seed for that years crops,

Tiegn and the Living Stones

that Vandil took the bull by the horns and came out of hiding by walking straight into Tiegn's hut and making himself at home.

Tiegn was too surprised to refuse him, but Lakiln who was also present prevented him from taking a seat and challenged him.

'So what evil brings you here where you are not wanted?' He asked. Vandil's recent exploits were well know by now from the Story Singers.

Vandil did not reply to this but turned to Tiegn. 'I still have a right by birth to be here don't I?' Tiegn felt that she had no choice—'Yes.' She said briefly. 'But since your evil association with Roondot you have shown that you are not to be trusted. Therefore whilst you are here you will be under my close authority and will report your actions every day at sun-down to Lakiln here. If there is any suggestion of your actions being contrary to that which Lakiln thinks is good for the Clan it will be reported to me and you will be estranged from the Clan. under my authority.'

She looked grimly at a very angry Vandil.

'Do you understand?, She insisted.

'Yes.' said Vandil briefly, and stormed out of the hut.

'Watch him.' Said Tiegn.

The daily activities of the Clan Chief had changed somewhat since the growth of the settlement. The most important facet of this new routine however remained that of a daily visit to

Tiegn and the Living Stones

the Stone Circle to commune with the ancestors just as her father Pandil had shown her how to do, as he himself had done, and as his father before him had done—back as far as anyone could remember.

This short ceremony needed someone to make the necessary preparations and it was inevitable that such a person would be intimately associated with the ruling Chief. In Tiegn's case it was her father's appointed assistant Betchen.

Betchen had no family having lost both parents in last winter's bout of the wasting illness. So as an only child he was now on his own and able to devote all his attention to Tiegn and her requirements. He was an attractive man, lean and strong. He was also very popular, enjoying his work he was a happy person always with a kind word for everyone. Exhibiting a natural intelligence he was often consulted for his wise judgement and honesty.

It was inevitable that there came an occasion when Betchan and Tiegn were alone together in the Ring of Stones that Tiegn became very aware of Betchan's physical presence.

The stirrings in her body were not to be denied so powerful were they. She had to acknowledge that he too seemed to look upon her differently,—his manner being both intimate and bold.

It was as if they shared some great secret.

Then almost but not quite accidentally their hands would touch and this sent a thrill through Tiegn. A thrill which slowly grew more intense.

Tiegn and the Living Stones

Then one day he was not waiting for her by the stone Circle to begin the morning procedures, and she suddenly became aware that Betchen meant more to her than she had dared to admit. Her relief when she saw his familiar figure striding towards her was almost overwhelming.

Then on a day which started out with a fine clear sky and brilliant sunshine which gave the giant stones a gentle sensual almost friendly feel, inviting one to stroke them. As usual there was only the two of them — The Chief and the Chief's assistant. The rest of the Clan was beginning to stir with just one or two early risers out and about. The short ceremony completed they sat on a flat stone side by side. Tiegn felt his proximity like a physical thing.

Suddenly on the pretext of reaching past her for some small item, Betchen let his hand gently caress her neck. That was all it took. The shock caused a fire to burn in her body. She gasped as it coursed down from her heart to her loins and she found it hard to draw breath. It seemed a long time before she recovered and became aware that Betchen had totally misunderstood her reaction and was busy stammering an apology.

'I am truly sorry,' he managed, 'for a moment I forgot that you are the Clan Chief. Er . . . it seemed as if I could not help myself.'

Tiegn managed a gentle smile and unable to speak for the turmoil still raging inside her, she placed one hand on his and looked into his eyes. Betchen held on to her hand and they simply sat smiling at each other. Betchen was finding it hard

Tiegn and the Living Stones

to believe that Tiegn might just feel about him what he had felt about her for some considerable time.

They were still at the Stones much later, when they re-gained some kind of control and not without some difficulty over their feelings. But for them both the feeling was of something bursting within them. Using words they had previously never previously dared, they poured out their feelings and both became aware of a deep almost irresistible driving force. With a terrible struggle Tiegn pushed him away and calmed down somewhat as she recognised that her place at the head of the Clan meant that she must behave with a great discretion. However, one thing was now supremely clear to both parties and that was that their feelings were mutual. This certainly was not a one sided thing, nor was it a brief passing attraction. It was, they knew, a factor which would govern their lives from now on.

Thus it was that two very sober and aware individuals got to their feet and made to leave the Stones that morning. A morning which neither of them would ever forget. But before they left Tiegn turned and knelt—and in a quiet but firm voice addressed the ancestors. She renewed her pledge of faith in them and asked them to take special care of this new-found relationship. The pair agreed to keep their feelings to themselves, as far as was possible.

Formal arrangements could wait and would be undertaken later.

But it did not quite turn out like that.

The Clans Folk noticed a change in their demeanour when they were together and their love became general knowledge.

And sure enough, Vandil realised that if the pair gave birth to a son he would never ever inherit the Chieftainship.

He had to do something about it. But what? Tiegn was popular, even loved. Whereas his own feelings were well known and suspicion would inevitably fall on him.

TIEGN TAKEN PRISONER

It seemed to be clear to Vandil that the key to his taking over as Chief was ownership of The Sword of Authority. With this famous instrument of power in his possession he would be able to stake his claim to the position, and it would be hard to deny him.

But he did not know who had taken it or where it was hidden. After discussing the problem with several of Tiegn's known supporters during which he alternately bullied them and offered them fat rewards, he was none the wiser. It was clear that they knew nothing of the sword's whereabouts.

Vandil had a puzzle.

Eventually he concluded that one person must know where the thing was. It seemed to him that it was essential that Tiegn must be able to put her hand on it should her position be challenged. She must know, he concluded.

It was essential that he grabbed the sword from her. However he could not do this alone. He needed troops. In this he had a problem in that almost all the Clans men would side with Tiegn against him.

He did not like the idea much, but he resolved to approach Roondot again. He had the manpower and such a force would not favour the Clan's folk.

It seemed to him that Tiegn had left him with no alternatives.

After all, she had turned down his suggestion of sharing the job of Chief.

'That was definitely not our father's wish.' She had said.

So on a day that was good for travelling, Vandil and a couple of staunch friends set off once more for Roondot territory.

Roondot was busy polishing his leather armour when Vandil's presence was announced.

They cleared all other folk away out of earshot.

Vandil wasted no time. 'I have a proposition for you.' He announced.

'One that I am certain you will be interested in.'

Roondot called a woman over and requested that she bring them some food and drink.

After they had eaten, Roondot having guessed what Vandil wanted started by making one or two things clear to him.

'As we experienced—out there,' he waved an arm round the horizon, 'I am greatly outnumbered and therefore any plan which suggests taking them on is out of the question.' He looked grimly at Vandil.

'Also I need to be convinced that whatever I am to get out of it—it will be worth my while.'

He smiled grimly—

'So tell me your idea.'

Vandil patiently explained the power that rested with the sword and that he thought that Tiegn must know where it was hidden.

'I need to get my hand on that symbol of high power.'

'If you agree to do this thing you must promise me that you will not harm her—especially if she divulges its whereabouts. If we harm her they will never cooperate no matter whether we have the sword or not.' He continued—

'When I am Chief I will pledge men to join you in whatever scheme you may have—in terms of numbers we would have more than any outside force.'

It seemed simple enough.

'Let me have a couple of days to consider matters, and I will let you know what I have decided.' Roondot said, dismissing Vandil with an abrupt wave of his hand.

Roondot thought deeply and concluded that it was worth a try, and so they got down to details.

Thus, several days later they put the plan into action.

Tiegn and the Living Stones

As was mentioned earlier—Tiegn was in the habit of walking over to the stones in the early dawn to share her thoughts with the ancestors. Usually the place was deserted which is why she chose such an hour.

There was a spell of fine days when the sun was high in the sky, even at that hour and only bird songs disturbed scene. This day was no exception.

Tiegn arrived at the stones alone.

As she made her way into the inner ring of stones, several men with faces covered to conceal their identities appeared from behind the stones and surrounded her. She was grabbed from behind and quickly tied with ropes, her head covered with a light woven cloth to prevent sight. She was then carried to a waiting horse and before anyone realised that their Chief had been captured and removed—they were gone. The troops divided and took several different ways back to base to confuse any would be followers.

Vandil stayed with the Clan and to still suspicion he organised several search parties to tramp the local areas—but not surprisingly without result.

QUESTIONS AND A SEARCH

Vandil was convinced that Tiegn must know where The Sword of Authority had been hidden and was therefore insistent that she was brought to no harm. A dead Tiegn was of no use whatsoever. He now put his own part of the plan into action.

He called a meeting of the full Clan.

It was another of those lovely balmy days, and word of the capture of Tiegn brought most of the Clans folk to the meeting. Vandil chose the inner ring.

He was confident of success and addressed the crowd with the firm authority that he now assumed.

'Folks of the Clan,' he began 'As you may have heard a rumour has been circulating that Tiegn has been captured by forces unknown. As far as I am concerned it is only a rumour, she may just have left to pursue some plan of her own.'

This was met with a disbelieving silence.

'However, as she is not here I have assumed the role of Clan Chief. That will remain the status until such time as Tiegn returns.'

This was met with an angry murmur.

'Why don't you go and find her?' said a voice in the crowd.

Vandil was expecting this.

'Because we have no idea where to look, it would be a total waste of man power.' He said.

'I bet Roondot knows where she is.' Said a voice in the crowd.

There was a round of approval at this.

Vandil waved an arm.

'I have decided.' He said. 'And that is final.'

'You do not have the sword.' Someone else shouted.

'Yes thank you for reminding me—I intend to instigate a search for it, starting immediately. And I will be coming round selecting men for the job.' —

'Thank you. That is all.'

And with that the people drifted away grumbling to themselves. The Clan was not a happy one.

Vandil also decided on a search of his own. There was someone who just might be able to suggest the whereabouts of the precious sword, and that person was the Clan seer Salin. He considered that if anyone should know of its whereabouts it must be she.

Therefore he planned to pay Salin a visit, but this gave him another problem—ever since he was small he was afraid of Salin. His mother, long since deceased, used to threaten him with Salin to scare him into doing that which he did not want to do.

Tiegn and the Living Stones

'If you don't finish your supper I will get Salin to turn you into a frog.'

Or something worse.

His common sense told him that his fears were groundless, but he couldn't rid himself of that wariness.

And so, one cloudy night with little or no moon, Vandil sneaked out of his hut and made his way silently into the surrounding trees. He chose to avoid any paths being guided by knife marks on the tree trunks which he had made several days previously. He arrived at Salin's neat hut and as he reached for the wooden door, Salin's voice called out—'Come on in, Don't be shy, I will not bite.'

He entered but until his eyes became accustomed to the gloom he could see little.

'I have been expecting you for some time,' Said Salin in a voice that commanded attention. 'You had better come up here where I can see you.' She said patting a stool which was just in reach of her hand.

'You are seeking the Sword of Authority in order to claim the position of Chief—and you think that I might know where it is?' She said when he was settled.

Vandil could only gape foolishly at this accurate analysis.

She waited.

'Well?' she said.

'By a process of elimination it seemed that it could only be you who had the courage and the

Tiegn and the Living Stones

know-how to take the thing and hide it.' Vandil said, to break the silence.

A standoff. They both knew that right or wrong, they would each never give in.

'You do know that I have the power to have you flogged and hung if you are telling lies.' Vandil said trying to frighten her.

To his surprise she laughed—'But without the sword you do not have the authority—and the Clan would prevent it.' She said.

And he knew that she was right.

As he left Salin she wondered if he knew that it was she who had hidden the sword, and that she was the only person who knew where it was. But she would die before divulging the information.

Vandil was not about to give up. The thing must be close by so that it could be retrieved almost instantly if it became necessary.

With this in mind he went around the Clan folk offering all manner of favours to anyone who would join in a search for the missing sword.

After several days Vandil had a dozen volunteer searchers and a day was chosen for the thing to begin.

Dawn broke grey and miserable but fortunately dry. The searchers were given their instructions. All the ground, every hut, and every person was to be subjected to the search starting at one edge of the cluster of huts and finishing at the far edge marked by the river. No-one was to be injured but the search must be

Tiegn and the Living Stones

thorough. In the event the Clans folk stood aside or volunteered to assist in the search.

At the end of a very long day with many disputes and several fights as searchers met sullen opposition there was still no sign of the sword.

In the absence of The Sword of Authority Vandil nevertheless began to assume the leadership of the Clan. He endeavoured to emulate his father Pandil's routines as well as those of Tiegn. He began by starting each day with contact with the ancestors as Tiegn had done many times. He was well aware that he was doing this despite his previous announcement that such action would be punished. But without the Sword what little power did his words hold?

It was clear to all that they wanted Tiegn back unharmed, especially Betchen—and just what was Vandil going to do about that little problem?

He was also very much afraid as to what Roondot might have in store for her.

Vandil was now in all kinds of trouble. It was soon to get even worse.

A SECRET FORCE

One Clan member, namely Betchen found that he could not stand by and watch the Clan be divided and destroyed especially now when the construction of the great double ring was so near to completion.

He began to put a plan in place which he had been considering for some considerable time. He set out to gather like minded folk and to form them into an organised opposition to Vandil and with the specific aim of rescuing Tiegn from Roondot's clutches and to reinstate her as Clan Chief.

This force started with just a few dedicated individuals, but as their intentions became known, a trickle of men and women wanting to join became a flood. At first they met and trained fighting techniques in secret, but this soon gave way to open meetings.

Betchen considered correctly that knowledge of the opposition force's existence would create fear in Roondot thus dissuading him from harming Tiegn whom he still held captive.

Then Vandil made a mistake, the first of many. Not realising the size or the determination of the opposition, he called yet another full Clan meeting. He stood before the assembled Clan and declared arrogantly that the opposition personnel were enemies of the Clan and told them that all those who remained in the opposition would be flung out of the Clan. At this unforgivable threat the opposition made themselves known and Vandil understood for the first time that he and his few followers were strictly outnumbered. He tried to threaten them—

'There are forces outside this Clan that I can and will call upon unless you accept my rule.'

This brought a roar of laughter, from an increasingly confident opposition.

To save what he could Vandil gathered his few men round him and marched off amidst jeers from the opposition troops.

'Don't rush back.'

'What! Giving up already?'

'Some Chief always running away.'

'You always were a coward.'

'Going to ask Roondot to hold your hand?'

But Betchen realised that when news of this confrontation got back to Roondot, that person would have to act. This would inevitably add a serious risk to Tiegn's life.

And sure enough Roondot challenged seriously for the first time since becoming Chief, decided on a final showdown. His plan was to put Tiegn on trial before her clan and subject her to torture in public until she gave them the whereabouts of the Sword of Authority. He was sure that ownership the Sword was the key to control of the Clans and of the Stone Circle. He was also confident that Tiegn would spill the beans.

It was important that Tiegn's Clan knew of this plan. He hoped that if Tiegn really did not have the information then the person who did have it would be forced to tell rather than watch her suffer. And so the day for the exposure was announced, and widely broadcast.

The day was stormy, the sky heavy with black clouds occasionally lit by distant lightening flashes and with an almost continuous rumble of thunder.

Teign's clan rolled up from every point of the compass, each of them armed with some simple weapon.

A wide circle of flat ground with a raised earth bank at its edge had been prepared and this was already overflowing with men.

At the circle's centre a fire burned brightly.

Roondot then understood that he was massively outnumbered. It was a mistake that he had made before and cursed himself for falling into the self same trap, but it was now far too late to withdraw.

There was too much noise for any speeches until Tiegn was escorted into the circle. Then an expectant hush descended on the crowd, and Roondot used it well.

'Friends.' He began, with deliberate irony. 'We are here to obtain justice.'

This raise an angry shout and jeers from the watching crowd.

Roondot tried to ignore this and continued—

'Vandil here has prime claim to an important symbol of Chieftainship—namely the Sword of Authority. And thus the Chieftainship itself.'

This raised a much louder even angrier shout.

It was some considerable time before he could continue, and his first words were drowned by an exceptionally loud clap of thunder. This subdued everyone present. Especially Roondot who thought that the storm was against him, possibly he thought it might have been raised by Salin.

But he had no choice but to press on. He had come this far and was committed.

'We believe that this person,' he indicated Tiegn with a casual wave of his hand, 'knows the whereabouts of this item and my man here with the red hot rod from the fire will press it into her flesh until she gives us the information that we require.'

Amidst a hail of boos he strode over to her and tore her robe from her shoulder and waved the man with the poker to go ahead.

Then it all happened so very quickly.

Betchen's squad, from a shout from him, invaded the circle, as a flash of lightening lit the scene with a terrible tearing noise as the very air was rent asunder.

The man with the poker got shoved into the fire and screamed as he tried to remove himself from the flames.

Roondot panicked, and realising that the vast majority were against him sneaked away under cover of the growing confusion.

Betchen grabbed Tiegn covered her with his cloak and using every dodge he knew half carried her through the midst of the rapidly advancing crowd.

In the melee that followed a single wildly thrown spear arced viciously through the air and descending struck Vandil in the chest.

It was a heavy weapon normally used for hunting big game and even with the protection of his leather armour the point drove in into the soft flesh between his ribs and pierced his heart. Vandil attempted to remove the weapon and very, very slowly crumpled to the earth where he lay still. No-one rushed to his aid and he lay where he fell unmoving.

The rain began to fall heavily.

He lay there, now quite dead.

Betchen having seen that Tiegn was safe, he and his troop gradually quietened the mob, but not without a fight with a few truculent Roondot supporters. But without their chief, Roondot's mob had had enough and loosing momentum, began to drift away in ones or twos.

With the main antagonists having left, the rest of the crowd gradually dispersed leaving a dead Vandil and a badly burned poker holder as the only serious casualties.

As the last individuals left, huge fingers of lightening lit the scene interspersed with deafening thunder. The burned man was helped away by his friends. Roondot was already safely far away.

As the storm abated, Tiegn seizing the opportunity began to use her authority to gain some control over her people and requested men to collect Vandil's body. She insisted that they treated him with the respect reserved for their honoured dead, to bring him home, and prepare his body for a formal burial.

Soon the view was empty of people, and the rain continued to fall incessantly.

Tiegn's heart was heavy as she considered that there would be some honest accounting to be done after this.

AN ACCOUNTING

Roondot on his return to his group found that his supporters had vanished. The people wanted peace and he was now regarded as a trouble maker. Another man altogether different from Roondot had assumed the job of chief. This Pern, as he was known, favoured peace over war and made it perfectly plain that Roondot was no longer welcome in their midst.

Roondot still had a mall group of dedicated followers who also found themselves no longer welcome.

In order to survive he came to the conclusion that his only way out was to form a military force and take over one of the smaller but successful clans.

Over some time he armed and trained his squad using the well known technique of mock battles. They formed a formidable fighting force.

However fate was against him, the Story singers had discovered what he was up to and had sung the news to all the local groups.

The heads of these groups got together and determined that if they defended themselves on a one against one basis Roondot would inevitably win, but if they all joined in they would field such a force many times more numerous than the enemy who would stand no chance whatsoever.

Tiegn and the Living Stones

So they practised responding to a call and together formed a formidable army capable of overwhelming Roondot's small troop. This they succeeded in keeping secret.

Inevitably the day came.

It was hot after heavy rain had turned the river into a flood and the ground was slippery with mud.

Scouts from the combined army reported that Roondot had gathered his force and was marching rapidly towards one of the smaller settlements. The defenders did a perfect job and a huge army of crudely armed men were waiting in the trees.

An unsuspecting troop with Roondot at its head marched blindly into the trap.

It was all over in a rush. On the shout of 'Charge' a huge horde quickly overwhelmed Roondot's tiny squad who were totally shaken by the wall of men charging angrily towards them. They did not wait to see what happened — they dropped their weapons and ran for their lives.

Roondot also made a run for it, but the only way not defended was towards the river. He thought that if he could get across he might get away.

The river however was in full flood from the recent rain.

Roondot reached the river bank and looked aghast at the boiling water as it roared between its steep banks. Without an alternative he jumped in and was soon lost to sight in the rushing waves.

He was never seen again. He had again fallen into the trap of being outnumbered, it seemed that he was unable to learn by his mistakes.

Back with Tiegn, the Story Singers arrived before Vandil's remains had been dealt with and told of the routing of Roondot and his troop. It was a propitious night and the entire Clan as seated round a grand fire. It was obvious that this was an historical occasion.

As the story unfolded the cheers became louder and almost continuous. It was soon obvious to all that peace now governed their lives.

There was a pause.

Then Salin dressed all in white stood up on the perimeter of the gathering. She was lit by the cold light of a full moon which seemed to hover just above her, giving her an un-earthly aspect. Then singing her own sweet song and carrying a sheaf of branches of bracken in her arms, she walked forward until she stood opposite the seated Tiegn. As her song ended she spoke to Tiegn in a clear voice that all should hear—

'I have here that which you should have, It will now be safe in your care. So I am thus returning it to its proper owner. My Chief. And the rightful Chief of this Clan.'

And throwing off the fronds that had hidden it, she held out with both her hands as if it was an offering to Tiegn—the Sword of Authority.

Tiegn and the Living Stones

That was it. The cheering lasted for an age. Everyone was pleased.

It was realised then that Salin had known of its whereabouts all the time at some risk to her life.

And then the Story Singers sang the history of the recent events.

They were four, two men and two women.

The first verse they sang and the whole Clan joined in the chorus.

The singers—
>   There was a man who wanted war,
>   He made an army fit to fight.
>   And stole our Chief, our shining star.
>   Then angered at her dreadful plight,
>   We had to act his plans to mar.

All—
>   This man was rotten
>   He will not be forgotten

The singers—
>   We had to rescue our Chief Tiegn.
>   Before a wounding did occur,.
>   Everyone who saw the sign.
>   Did their best to cherish her.
>   The first one of our time.

All—
>   This man was rotten,
>   He will not be forgotten.

Tiegn and the Living Stones

This song was well received and was sung many times through the evening and long into the night. No one in the clan could remember such an occasion of celebration.

But a more serious note claimed their attention. Before the party broke up Tiegn stood in front of the whole Clan and waited for the noise of many conversations to cease. She appeared to be frail her slender frame in its white cloak small against the dark shapes of the giant stones. But when she slowly spoke the words, there was no mistaking their authority.

'We thank our friends the Story Singers who have given us an evening to remember. You will always be welcome here as long as I am Chief.'

This raised a loud and prolonged cheer.

'But sadly starting at dawn tomorrow we have a sad duty to perform. We must bury my unfortunate half brother Vandil. I believe him to have been wrongly advised, but he was of my household and will therefore be interned in the same grave as my father whose son he was. It would please me if some of you could see your way to forgiving him his lapse and attend the short ceremony.'

There was a low murmer from the assembled Clan.

'And so I bid you all good might and may the ancestors look over us.'

As she turned to leave, someone stood up in the crowd and shouted —

'Give a cheer for our Chief Tiegn and long may she be there.'

She bowed to the crowd, and was suddenly surrounded by well wishers.

It was a personal triumph.

Dawn broke dull and drear. Vandil's body had been prepared overnight, and the grave opened.

As Tiegn made her way to the grave she was cheered by the large number of the Clan who had turned up. In her arms she carried the Sword of Authority.

Lakiln stood and said the words that committed Vandil to the soil.

Tiegn made to kiss the corpse, turned to the pale sun just visible through the grey clouds. And in a clear ringing voice declaimed—

'Go to our ancestors my brother you will answer to their higher authority for your actions, and not to us.'

And with that they all left the place except the grave diggers, and the daily work of the Clan got under way.

Jml
18/01/2013

LIST OF CHARACTERS

Pandil	-	Father to daughter Tiegn and son Vandil Chief of the Clan
Tiegn	-	Daughter of Pandil by his first wife. By Clan law rightful new Chief of the Clan
Vandil	-	Son of Pandil by his second wife,
Lakiln	-	Tiegn's loyal Deputy
Spell Wellan Salleter	} - }	Three men with views on what to do with the small stones
Bork	-	Some considerable time earlier tried to destroy the stone circles
Sonlith	-	An earlier Chief
Jan	-	Pandil's second wife and Vandil's mother
Salin	-	The Clan's official seer
Roondot	-	Chief of aggressive Clan

Betchen	-	Close friend of Teign's
Sentin	-	Stone worker
Wellin	-	Stentin's son
Shelly	-	Sentin's partner
Shell	-	Sentin's daughter
Style	-	Shell's lover from Roondot's Clan
Pern } Thenmgis }	-	Roondot's men
Red	-	The lad who rode the boar

ABOUT STONEHENGE

This story describes just one way that this famous monument may have played a part in the lives of those dedicated people who prepared and raised these giant Stones and those who supported them in this endeavour.

To achieve what they did must have demanded considerable manpower, which in its turn meant that there had to be a gathering of quite a substantial number of permanent dwellings. The driving force behind all this activity can only be guessed at, but in any event it must have been tremendously powerful. The assumption behind this version of events is that it stems from a relationship of the living with their ancestors. In any case we can only look upon this great monument with wonder and admiration for those who built it.

The truth is that we may never know.

JML